The storm broke with a lashing violence....

Between the great booms of thunder and gusts of wind that rattled the shutters, Diane could hear every creaking in the old house. She jumped when three sharp knocks sounded at the dining-room window. Mystified, she was more curious than afraid and hurried to open the shutters.

A tall, well-built young man was silhouetted against the night. A streak of lightning flashed, followed by a crash of thunder, and then all the lights went out.

For a moment Diane stood frozen. She was alone in the house, except for the servants. Should she let the stranger in?

Other

MYSTIQUE BOOKS

by CORIOLA

61 INTRIGUE IN MOROCCO

Stranger at Midnight

by CORIOLA

MYSTIQUE BOOKS

TORONTO · LONDON · NEW YORK

STRANGER AT MIDNIGHT/first published April 1980

Copyright © 1980 by Worldwide Library.
Copyright © MCMLV by Librairie Jules Tallandier,
as LE VOYAGEUR DE LA NUIT
Philippine copyright 1980. Australian copyright 1980.
ISBN 0-373-50073-4

PRINTED IN U.S.A.

Chapter 1

With a large basket under her arm, Diane moved quietly through the garden, pruning those geraniums that had faded and wilted in the hot sun. She loved this time of day, when the air was heavy with the sweet scent of flowers and the sun was slowly slipping beneath the horizon.

On the lush, green lawns, the long shadows of twilight stretched out like slim, dark fingers pointing to the cool, dim woods that echoed with the faint rustle of wings and the soft twitter of birds as they returned to their nests for the night. From a nearby hedge came the plaintive cry of a bullfinch, and deep within the woods, the gentle cooing of a wild turtledove lingered softly in the gathering dusk. Each bird's song rang out distinctly in the stillness of the approaching evening.

Suddenly Diane caught the whiff of freshly cut hay and, for a moment, straightened from her bending position to inhale its tangy fragrance, her nostrils quivering with pleasure. As she stood there, her eyes moved across the countryside that stretched out before her, swathed in a bluish haze.

Slowly she turned around and looked fondly at the sturdy old house with its wide, brown, tiled roof. It was a good house, she thought, strong, stalwart. It seemed to mock the passing of the years, to keep the forest at bay with the sheer strength of its personality. Sure and proud, it sat on its solid foundation, a monument to its quiet victories over the passing centuries. Behind it, the stately trees stood in all their majesty.

Black Oaks. Who had named it, she wondered. Diane knew that the name dated from 1660 and that apparently the house—the estate—had never been called anything else. And the Bernards had always lived at Black Oaks. An old neighbor had once told her that her family was a fixture in the area just like the old house they lived in. *Yes*, Diane thought, *we're a venerable old family, as intrinsic a part of the area as the sharp curve at the end of the road. But what's left of us now? Two women, that's all.*

She sighed. Well, there might be just the two of them, but the love that she and her grandmother shared for this old estate made them both determined that it would survive and prosper for yet another generation of Bernards.

As Diane returned her attention to the geraniums, she thought objectively about her grandmother. How did the older woman appear to others, she wondered. Well, Mrs. Bernard was tall and imposing, with severe features softened only slightly by the snow-white hair that framed her face.

So much for the visual description, Diane murmured to herself, *but what do people think of my grand-*

mother? Did they see her as a severe, single-minded woman, one who was both inflexible and unyielding? Oh, surely not. Certainly, everyone who knew her had the utmost respect for her, and if she was a little severe, surely they realized that it was because of her tremendous love for Black Oaks and the enormous amount of work she had to put into its upkeep.

Diane marveled at her grandmother's energy. The Black Oaks estate was vast. Diane remembered becoming lost in its forests time after time as a little girl. She used to be wholly convinced she'd wandered miles away from home. And so she had, in a way. When the little girl would eventually be discovered by one of the farmhands, the house would, indeed, be a considerable distance away, even though her short legs had not carried her anywhere near the estate's boundaries. Mile after mile of land stretched out around the large manor house. The larger part of it was forested and supported both a carefully controlled logging operation and valuable hunting reserves, but several hundred acres close to the house were farmed. *And grandmother*, Diane thought, a proud smile coming to her lips, *manages every bit of it.*

Suddenly the sound of footsteps on the garden path interrupted her thoughts, and she turned around to see her grandmother's silhouette outlined in the last rays of the setting sun. Diane put down her pruning shears and, brushing a geranium leaf from her hand, went to meet the older woman.

"Hello, grandmother," she said, shading her eyes with one hand. "Have you come to watch the sunset with me? It's such a lovely evening, why don't we sit in the garden for a while? The flowers are really lovely, now."

"Have you finished pruning the geraniums, dear?"

"Almost," Diane replied. "They'll be all done tomorrow."

They sat down side by side on a stone bench along the fence and basked in the silence of the early evening, which was broken every now and then by sounds of frogs croaking in the nearby pond.

"How did it go today?" Diane asked softly, moving her head in the direction of the farm. The overseer's house and several outbuildings were clearly visible over the garden fence, which was sturdy enough to keep out wandering livestock.

"We'll never change some of those farmhands," Mrs. Bernard replied wearily. "I got there today just in time to catch Beauval putting two sacks of wheat in his wagon. He's one of several of the men who are constantly trying to make more money by selling a little of my grain on the side. It's incredible. I've caught them at it and stopped them several times, but what bothers me is how often they've actually managed to get away with it."

"It's too bad you can't find some way of stopping the whole thing." Diane commented sympathetically. "Why don't you just fire them all and hire new people?"

"Maybe at the end of this season I'll get rid of the bad apples," Mrs. Bernard replied. "Heaven knows, I've got plenty of reason to let them go. For the first three years after your grandfather's death it wasn't too bad. But this year it's getting completely out of hand. That overseer, Gerardy, must know about it, but he claims he can't prevent it, either.

"Really, it's too much," the old woman sighed. "They know I have the lumber business to run, too, and I can't spend the whole day watching them, so they take advantage of my absence to steal whatever they can. Some of them don't respect my authority at all anymore. Well, that's not quite true," she added. "They're still afraid of getting a good clout from my cane."

"Did you tell them I saw some cows in the woods the other day?"

"Yes I did. And do you know what they said? That the cows escaped from the pasture all by themselves. I told them right then and there that if they ever let the stock wander again, I would call in the police and let the law deal with them. I've overlooked a lot of things, but that was the last straw. I just won't tolerate that kind of neglect of duty, and I told them so.

"I think they got the message," Mrs. Bernard added, clasping her bony hands on her lap. "I've concentrated so much time and effort on the lumber business, I'm afraid the farming has suffered as a consequence. But I guess it's been worth it."

For a few minutes the two women sat together in companionable silence. In the gathering dusk, soft breezes carrying the fragrance of freshly cut hay, blew gently in from the nearby fields.

"You know, it's a constant battle, a never-ending struggle against failure," the older woman continued softly. "A fight to the finish, that's what it is. You can't let up for one minute. And you can never allow yourself the luxury of saying, 'Well, I'm just too tired today.' We have to keep on reminding ourselves we can win. And we will . . . we must."

"Let's go in," she said suddenly, placing her hand gently on Diane's arm. "It's getting a little chilly."

The interior of the house evoked the same feeling as the outside, Diane thought. It always gave her the impression that it had been built for strong, rugged men who needed space and a kind of rough grandeur around them. It was a house for rough and ready hunters, plain-spoken hearty men who took life as it came.

The huge main hall was tiled with great slabs of gray flagstone. In the large dining room was an enormous rough-hewn beam that extended the full length of the ceiling. Its middle was marked by two deer carved in the wood, silent witnesses to the long years of history that had passed before them in that very room. Like the hall, the dining room was tiled with huge slabs of gray stone, worn thin over the years by an endless stream of footsteps.

A long narrow table made of a single piece of thick wood stood in the middle of the room. The beautiful brown wood was smooth to the touch with the warm glow of centuries in its soft sheen. Some of the little square windows, set back into the thick walls, looked out toward the front of the house. Others peered onto an enclosed veranda at the side, a fairly recent addition to the rambling structure.

The table had already been set for dinner. Place settings of silver and delicate crystal provided a dramatic contrast with the rich dark wood.

Diane walked quickly across the room toward the table, her two Irish setters following close at her heels. She held herself very erect as she moved, her long, ash blond hair falling softly around her shoulders. She looked very young with her thin, delicate face and silky hair, but there was a serious, at times even somber, expression in her clear, bright eyes.

She took her place at the long table beside her grandmother. Old Mrs. Bernard looked a very imposing
figure as she presided over the dining room; she was
dignified—almost regal. But Diane had never been
intimidated in any way by her grandmother, who had
been the major figure in her life almost as long as she
could remember.

The two women chatted easily through dinner, most
of the conversation centering on their mutual interest
and love—Black Oaks. But though the conversation
was light in tone, Diane noticed with concern that her
grandmother seemed more tired than usual, that there
was a strained look on that well-loved, lined face. She
refrained from commenting, however, knowing her
grandmother well enough to hold her peace until the
older woman chose to broach the subject of her worry.

During dessert, Germaine, one of the old family retainers, came into the dining room and spoke quietly to
her mistress. "Charles would like to speak to you,
ma'am."

"Charles? At this hour? All right, have him come in,"
Mrs. Bernard said, glancing quickly over at her granddaughter.

"Maybe he wants to talk to you about the poachers,"
Diane remarked. "I told him that when I was walking
in the woods this morning, I heard a shot that seemed
to come from the direction of Clearwater Springs."

At that moment, Charles walked in, holding a spool
of wire in his hand. Charles, who was married to
Marthe, the cook, was technically the estate's gamekeeper and general overseer of its grounds, but his long
service had made him familiar with most aspects of the
operations, and Mrs. Bernard relied on him for many

things. His loyalty to her was great, and his love of
Black Oaks all but equaled that of the owner herself.
But he was getting older and was less and less able to
get around the huge estate. However, he was in good
physical shape for his age and generally carried his
seventy-two years well.

"That's part of an animal trap you've got there, isn't
it, Charles?" Mrs. Bernard asked sharply.

"It sure is," he replied. "I nearly ended up like one of
the animals, too," he laughed.

"What do you mean?" Diane asked. "Sit down and
tell us what happened."

"Well, there are at least four poachers," he began. "I
just spotted them a while ago. Judging by their equipment, they're professionals, too, not just men from the
village hoping to snag a rabbit or two."

The old man looked intently at Mrs. Bernard. "If we
don't do something, they're going to kill a lot of
animals in the reserve. I nearly got caught in one of
their blasted deer traps myself. It was just getting dark,
and I couldn't see my way too clearly in the woods.
Fortunately, I saw a branch lying across the path and
caught a glimpse of a piece of bent wood in the bushes.
I walked over to it and untied it, then, whoosh, it
snapped back like a whip. You best take care, Miss
Diane, when you go walking in the woods. You could
get caught in one of those things."

Mrs. Bernard threw a quick look at her granddaughter. "Yes, be very careful about walking in the woods
for a while, do you hear, Diane?" she said. "I'd hoped
we wouldn't have to face this problem again—not for a
while at least. Professional poachers are insidious, and
the woods are likely to be riddled with their traps."

"All right, grandmother, I'll be careful. But what are we going to do? We can't let them get away with it," she replied. "A gang of determined poachers could destroy the reserve if we don't stop them."

"I know that, dear. And of course we'll do something about it," she said brusquely. "We haven't had any persistent poaching in the forest since years before your grandfather died—and I don't propose to let the situation continue. But you and I aren't the ones to deal with something like this."

"I'll do the best I can, Mrs. Bernard—" Charles began.

"No, Charles," the old woman interrupted firmly. "I won't have it. I know what happens to a man who goes out there in those woods alone in situations like this. And anyway, what could you do against a whole group of them? There's only one solution. We'll have to inform the game wardens and the police. After all, illegal hunting is a serious offense in this jurisdiction."

"Why don't we ask Leo what he thinks we should do," Diane suggested. "We could talk to him about it and tell him what's going on. I'm sure he'd have some ideas."

"Of course," the older woman exclaimed. "An excellent suggestion. Yes, we could certainly ask him for help. He loves a good fight and would enjoy tracking down those poachers."

A slight smile hovered on Diane's lips when she thought of Leo Marchand. He was a neighbor and trusted friend of the family, and for the past three months he had been her fiancé.

"I meant we should talk to him about it. I don't think we can really count on his being able to do anything for us right now," she remarked. "He's completely wrapped up in preparations for the horse show. He can't think of anything else."

"But he's still coming over for lunch tomorrow, isn't he?" her grandmother asked anxiously.

"Oh, yes, that's still on."

"Well, we'll discuss the problem with him then. I trust that young man a great deal, and it wouldn't be a bad idea for him to start involving himself in the running of Black Oaks," she said.

The old woman looked over at Charles. "We could both use some young ideas. I don't want my forests ruined by those thieves, and if I have to lie in wait for them myself.... Well, it isn't a question of stooping to their tactics—at least, not yet," she added softly.

LATER THAT NIGHT, Diane stood gazing out her bedroom window. Against the stormy sky, she could see the shadows of the great stately trees, their branches moving softly in the night breeze. She could hear all kinds of noises coming from the surrounding land, and knowing it as well as she did, she could identify almost every one of them. She liked the feeling of being the only one up when everyone else was sleeping.

Diane let her thoughts wander. She loved the estate profoundly and knew how desperately difficult it was becoming to make ends meet. The enormous house was costly to maintain, and even though the domestic staff, which consisted mostly of faithful old retainers, had been cut to the bare minimum needed to handle the chores, the payroll was burdensome.

The farm was also proving expensive. For the past three years, the crops had been severely hit by uncontrollable plagues of insects and unusually scanty rainfall and had not yielded profitable harvests. Taxes kept going up, and so did the cost of seed, fertilizer and shipping. Unexpected replacements had had to be made among the livestock. The various farm buildings seemed constantly in need of repair. With pilfering and now poaching added to all these problems, Diane knew that her grandmother must be at her wit's end to balance the books.

Still, if the poaching could be curtailed, Diane thought optimistically, that might help a little. Leo might help there. He rarely seemed to work up much interest in the problems of Black Oaks, but surely if she and her grandmother both asked him, Leo might have time for this very serious one....

Leo: her fiancé—the man she was going to marry. *I shouldn't have agreed to marry him*, Diane thought, *at least not yet.*

It wasn't that she didn't love him, she told herself, it was just that he was...was what? Why was she hesitant about her engagement to Leo, she wondered. Why the misgivings? Certainly he was attractive. He had been a neighbor almost all Diane's life at Black Oaks and was as familiar as she with the estate. He was an excellent horseman; indeed, he cut a very dashing figure in his tight jodhpurs and long black riding boots. His blue eyes would laugh down at her, and his tanned face would break into a confident smile.

But something in Leo's attitude disturbed Diane. She caught herself thinking that he behaved as if he were playing a part. He seemed to see himself as a handsome cavalier riding into her life and sweeping her off her feet. And cavalier was certainly the word to describe his attitude toward her and her beloved Black Oaks. It was as if he was laughing at her fierce love of the estate and mocked her efforts to help her grandmother in the arduous task of keeping it running.

Diane wondered if her grandmother saw this in Leo. Or was she too beguiled by his charming smile and gallantry?

Diane sighed as she walked away from the window to her bed. Mrs. Bernard had been very pleased by the match between Leo and her granddaughter, seemed almost to have promoted it. Perhaps the old lady was anxious to transfer the management to younger hands and to see a new generation of Bernards before her life was over.

When Diane finally fell asleep, it was to the image of Leo's face thrown back in laughter, his eyes sparkling with mockery.

Chapter 2

The next morning, as Diane was brushing her hair, she thought suddenly of the poachers. Charles had said there were four of them, she remembered with a shiver. Four of them with their vicious traps, just waiting to kill all those beautiful animals. And if it had been poachers she'd heard the day before, shooting some- where around Clearwater Springs, they were bold enough to use guns, too.

They must have come to Black Oaks because they knew the reserves of game in the forest were plentiful, she thought. Perhaps they also knew the estate's game- keeper was old and couldn't run fast enough to catch them, not to mention the fact that the forest was so enormous that the chances of their being caught by even the most nimble pursuer were remote.

Well, she was going to help the old man out, Diane decided, and together, they would put a stop to the poaching once and for all. . . .

When she passed the study on the way to the dining

room she heard her grandmother engaged in conversation with Gerardy, the supervisor of the farmhands. First thing every morning, the two got together to discuss the work to be done that day. As Diane listened to her grandmother and the overseer hash out matters that were all too familiar to her, she couldn't help but smile at the older woman's positive attitude, her keen foresight and the precise authoritative manner with which she expressed her ideas.

The man with Mrs. Bernard was tall and strong with a smug look on his face. He was very sure of himself and only half listened to the older woman, nodding impatiently and interrupting her rudely from time to time. However, Diane was quite sure that he was aware Mrs. Bernard knew just as much about farming as he did and that he went along with all her suggestions only because his contract of employment required him to.

"...there was no excuse whatsoever for those cattle getting loose and trampling that field, Gerardy. Why wasn't the gate made secure?"

"I told you the wood was rotten, Mrs. Bernard," the overseer replied insolently. "It was only a matter of time before the cattle broke through. Gimme some decent wood, and I'll fix 'er up okay."

"Give you license to pillage the forest, you mean," Diane heard her grandmother reply tartly. "Well, Gerardy, I'll strike you a bargain. While I do not believe the cattle knocked down the gate—they're hardly aggressive animals—I am prepared to concede that that wood is getting old and the fencing could use some repairs. I will inform Charles and he can accompany you when you choose the trees to be chopped down."

After Gerardy left, the old woman came into the dining room, where Diane was finishing her coffee.

"That man's always trying to catch me up on one thing or another," her grandmother remarked. "He pretends he doesn't understand what I want, but I know he does. He would be a complete idiot if he didn't know what I expect by now."

"I don't like the look of that man," Diane replied. "And I wish his contract didn't have him live on the property. His wife is even worse than he is. I think that she encourages her husband to be insolent. It's as if he feels that grandfather was the real boss, and ever since he died four years ago, Gerardy hasn't been willing to concede that you've taken over."

"It's too bad we can't seem to trust one another," the older woman said pensively. "After all, our interests are really the same: his contract calls for him to receive a percentage of the farm's profits—when there are any. He is a very good farmer, but I'm still thinking of replacing him, next year. I can't prove enough against him to justify breaking his contract now, but I can't help suspecting he turns a blind eye to the men's pilfering. Maybe he's even in on it himself, though he'd never let me catch him."

"You'd think the men would be content with what you pay them," Diane remarked. "You certainly put out an enormous sum in wages each month, especially during the summer season."

"I guess they feel that what they steal from me almost doubles their salaries," responded her grandmother.

"Do they really steal that much?"

"No, but it's what they try for. Charles, fortunately, keeps a close eye on them. They don't know he's watching them, of course, but he is. He's a farmer's son and knows all the tricks of the trade. Between the two of us, there's not much that happens around here that we don't know about. We make a good team, if I do say so myself," she added smiling quietly to herself.

After a brief pause, Mrs. Bernard continued wryly, "When your grandfather died, the men were counting on my age. They thought they could fool a silly old woman with their shennanigans, but they didn't take into account how tough I can be when it come to protecting your interests, dear."

"And what about the poachers?" Diane asked suddenly.

"That's still bothering you, eh? Well, Charles is going to take care of all that."

"Have you talked with him already this morning?"

"I most certainly have. I want to get this matter cleared up as soon as possible. After thinking the situation over, I realized there's a good chance the root of the trouble is one of the lumberjacks. If those poachers aren't from around here—and, somehow, I don't think they are—then one of the lumberjacks would be their most likely contact. It would be quite easy for him because he'd know the pattern of movement in the forest. And he'd be right on the spot to receive the stolen goods and then sell them elsewhere."

"But if that's what's happening, what can we do about it?" asked Diane. "They work so deep in the forest."

"We'll have to get them all together and question them," answered her grandmother. "I've sent Charles to tell the foremen what's going on. If it is one of the lumberjacks, then we'll find him and send him packing right away. And that will be the end of it."

"It's not going to be easy to find him," Diane said thoughtfully.

"No, it won't be. If I'd been able to afford two or three good assistant gamekeepers working to assist Charles, those poachers wouldn't have come in the first place. Enough gamekeeprs would have been able to take the proper precautions and we wouldn't be in the fix we are today. But that kind of thinking doesn't get us anywhere, does it? However, I'm not too worried. Charles is a good man and knows his job. He'll help us all he can. And I think the lumber foremen can be trusted. And I've also notified the Federation of Game Wardens. And if I have to get out there and help them find these people myself, I will."

Diane threw a quick glance at her grandmother. *Nothing would surprise me about this woman*, she thought. For years, Mrs. Bernard had been one of the best shots in the country, and in spite of her age, Diane knew she wouldn't hesitate to defend Black Oaks personally, if required.

Diane looked at the old woman affectionately. "I'm with you all the way, grandmother," she said warmly. "When Charles gets back, we'll put our heads together and see what we can come up with. If necessary, we'll all go after those poachers," she added as she patted the silky coat of the Irish setter lying quietly at her feet.

"Well," the older woman sighed. "I better see how Marthe is getting along in the kitchen. She is terribly upset with all this talk of poachers. She's afraid Charles might get hurt—as if he didn't know how to take care of himself by now. Also, I want to make sure she doesn't burn the sweet and sour cabbage we're having for lunch. It's one of Leo's favorite dishes."

"I'm going to finish pruning back the geraniums now," Diane said getting up from the table. "Then I'll go to meet Leo. I can take the dogs with me and give them a little run at the same time."

The sun was bright and warm as Diane collected her pruning shears and basket from the gardening shed. It was a beautiful day, and the garden was looking its best. As Diane worked, pruning the geraniums, she felt a contentment settle upon her. The garden was her pride and joy, and she spared no effort on its behalf.

Some time later she stood back from the flowers to ease her back and glanced at her watch. With a gasp she realized that two hours had flown by; if she was going to meet Leo, she would have to tidy up quickly.

Not five minutes later, Diane walked out the front door, her scruffy jeans replaced by a blue and white sundress. Long hours of gardening and walking in the estate had turned her skin to gold, and her long, blond hair was very pale from the sun's bleaching.

Diane moved gracefully as she walked down the long driveway to the gates at the end of the farm. She whistled to the setters, and they came bounding along beside her as if they were as happy as she in the hot midday sun. The beauty of the surroundings and the joy she always derived from the garden had made Diane forget her anxieties about the estate for the moment.

She recognized the sound of Leo's car before she saw it, and she waited for it to come up over the crest of the small hill that marked the boundary of the estate grounds. She whistled for her dogs and walked over to an old oak tree where she stood in the shadow of the enormous branches that stretched up toward the sky. In contrast to the huge tree, she seemed delicate, almost fragile.

As Leo drove nearer, he must have seen her through the leaves of the great oak. Diane had no idea the lovely picture she made standing beneath the huge branches, her two dogs lying quietly at her feet.

"Hi, darling!" Leo called cheerfully through his car window. "Isn't it a marvelous day? The only thing missing was you, so now it's complete," he exclaimed. "Let me just park the car."

He drove past Diane to park the car in front of the house. By the time he'd finished, Diane had retraced her steps and was standing on the steps of the house ready to greet him properly.

"Darling," he said again, as he held her in his arms, his chin resting on top of her ash blond head. "I'm so happy. If you could see how well Golden Boy is responding to training, you would be amazed. You'll be proud of both of us, just wait and see." He buried his face in her hair and kissed her.

Diane had known he would start talking about his work with his horses right away. He never talked about anything else, really, she thought. He was always like that: only interested in the things that concerned him, accustomed to being the center of attention. . . .

"Is Golden Boy jumping well?" she asked, hoping to please him by her interest.

"He's not a horse," Leo said proudly, "he's a bird. He flies, Diane. He just glides over those hurdles. He's elegant, graceful. You've got to see him, he's fantastic."

"My, it's beautiful out today," he went on enthusiastically. "Let's take a walk around the garden, shall we?
That will give me a chance to tell you what I've been
doing this past week."

Diane nodded her head in agreement. "And...I...I
have some things I want to tell you, too," she said hesitantly.

"Of course. You know how interested I am in Black
Oaks."

"Well, do you want to start or shall I?" she asked.

"Begin, begin," he said. "Then you won't be dis-
tracted when I tell you my news."

"But what about you? What did you want to tell
me?" she persisted.

"Never mind that now. Tell me your news. I'm all
ears."

"Well, we've got some poachers in the forest. They're
stealing a lot of our deer. Charles was almost caught in
one of their traps the other night."

"There are poachers in every forest, Diane," Leo
replied offhandedly. "Is that why you have such a long
face all of a sudden? Because of some silly poachers?"
he asked in surprise.

"I'm worried about our hunting reserves," she went
on, slightly irritated because he wasn't taking the problem seriously. "It's not only that they're valuable. Do
you think I spent all last winter helping Charles carry
hay and rock salt miles into the forest for the deer just
so those thieves could come around and steal them
whenever they felt like it?"

"You shouldn't feel that all the work you and Charles
did was in vain; it was a worthwhile endeavor. So there
are some poachers hanging around. They won't stay

long, and even if they do, they won't take all the animals."

"But, Leo," she cried, her voice beginning to quiver, "we haven't had any serious trouble with poachers since grandfather died. If we just sit back and let them move in on us now, they could ruin the reserves we've built up, and there wouldn't be any more good hunting in our forest for a long time, maybe never."

"Charles is pretty smart—he'll catch them. Don't worry. They aren't the first poachers and they won't be...."

"Charles is an old man. He can't do it all by himself," Diane retorted heatedly. "We've got to help him."

"Hey, relax, Diane. Getting excited won't solve anything. You fret too much," he said, putting his arm around her. "Take your mind off Black Oaks for a while. I want to see a smile on your face."

"Okay, it's your turn now," she said, resolutely pushing the poachers to the back of her mind. "Tell me everything you've been doing. We can talk about the poachers later with grandmother and decide on the best course of action."

For the rest of their walk, Leo talked of nothing but his tremendous success with training his horses and his hopes for the coming horse show. Diane couldn't help smiling as she listened to him. Golden Boy was going through all his paces without a single fault, clearing the stone wall, the stream, even the verge. He was performing like a dream with all Leo's hopes riding on him. The animal hadn't let his owner down once.

"He's a real show horse, Diane. I know I can get him to jump the two meters. Then I'm going to try my luck at the big competitions."

"And what about your parents? What do they think about all this?"

"Well, dad's still going on at me to go into the lumber business," Leo replied easily. "But he's been doing that ever since I convinced him I really wasn't going to follow in his footsteps as a lawyer. I think he's beginning to change his mind."

"What about your mother?"

"Oh, mother is very supportive. She understands that horses are my life and that I'd never be any good managing lumber—or anything else for that matter. But I need encouragement from you, Diane," he said suddenly, whirling around to face her. "I need to know that you're behind me all the way, that you support me." Leo held Diane by her shoulders, his grip getting tighter as he spoke.

Diane was amazed at the urgency in his voice. "Yes, yes, I promise," she laughed. "I'll encourage you all I can. But, Leo, this is a very expensive hobby you've chosen for yourself, isn't it?" she asked in a more serious tone of voice.

"Hobby?" he exclaimed indignantly. "What do you mean, 'hobby'? You sound like my father when you talk like that. I'm serious about this, Diane. I'm involved with horses because I love the work and also because people are rediscovering horses these days and there's plenty of money to be made in them.

"Now," he continued, suddenly very serious but with a note of excitement in his voice, "since you're the only one who really knows how I feel about all this, I'm going to let you in on a little secret. I have very definite plans for the future. I'm going to raise and breed horses. Well, don't look so surprised, and for heaven's sake don't tell anyone yet. I'm hoping to persuade my father to clear that little oak grove behind our house. We could get a lot of money from the sale of all those trees, and I could use some of it to build a beautiful training ground."

"Cut down that beautiful oak grove?" she murmured.

"Darling, just think about it for a minute," Leo said a little impatiently. "A healthy little profit could be made from the sale of that wood. And with that money, I could buy a lot of the equipment I need, and dad would still have a tidy sum left over for himself."

"But don't you think you should talk to grandmother about your plans?" she said hesitantly. "I mean, she's counting on you to help run Black Oaks."

"Breeding horses won't interfere with my running Black Oaks," he replied confidently. "She knows I'll give her all the help she needs. You know that too, don't you, Diane?"

"Yes, Leo," she said slowly. "But we did agree to live at Black Oaks after we are married, remember?"

"Of course, darling," he assured her, smiling brightly. "It's only eight miles from Black Oaks to my place. That's nothing. Besides, I'll have a manager staying over at Wildacres looking after things for me. And here at Black Oaks, I'll have my lovely wife. What a wonderful life we're going to have together, my sweet. Of course, you'll have to get involved too, you know."

"Involved with what? You mean with training horses?"

As Leo was about to reply, both of them caught sight of old Mrs. Bernard walking out to join them. Quickly he said to Diane, "Don't say anything about my plan, darling, promise? We'll discuss it later."

Diane was perplexed by the mystery her fiancé insisted on surrounding his scheme with, but before she had had a chance to comment, he had walked over to meet her grandmother.

"Good day, Mrs. Bernard. You're looking well—and beautiful as usual."

Diane found herself smiling at Leo's wily charm. As she followed the other two into the house though, she wondered how he would respond to her grandmother's plea for help against the poachers.

Chapter 3

"How are your parents, Leo?" Mrs. Bernard asked, serving him some sweet and sour cabbage.

"In very good form, as a matter of fact, Mrs. B," Leo replied cheerily.

"Of course, I don't see much of father. He seems to spend most of his time at the office. To be quite honest with you, I think he's avoiding me. He's certainly getting a little stingy about my allowance. I think he feels that if he cuts off some of my money, I'll be induced to settle down to a career and move out of the house."

"Does he still want you to go into the lumber business?"

"I guess so. He doesn't seem to realize that if Golden Boy gets some wins, I'll have some money coming in from that."

"I'm sure he would understand, if you explained it to him, Leo," Mrs. Bernard returned mildly.

"He says I'm being a dilettante," Leo said, his tone clearly indicating his exasperation with his father. "I think he's never really forgiven me for not finishing my law studies at the university. He thinks only sons have to follow in the old man's footsteps and all that sort of thing."

"And how is your mother?" Mrs. Bernard asked, tactfully sidestepping what she knew was a delicate subject.

"Oh, she's fine. Spending all father's hard-earned money, as usual. I swear she goes to Paris once a week and comes back every time with boxes and boxes of clothes. And you know, she's redecorating the living room again. It was done only two years ago! But she says now that using green was a mistake. It makes her seasick!" Leo threw his head back in laughter, and Diane noticed her grandmother chuckling, a rare sight.

"So what color is it going to be now?" Diane asked in amusement.

"Peaches and cream, to use mother's expression. She thinks it will look prettier in the sunset!"

The conversation was interrupted as Marthe entered the dining room unexpectedly. "Excuse me, ma'am, I don't mean to barge in on you like this, but I'm starting to get really worried," she said to her mistress in a low but concerned tone. "Charles has been gone since eight this morning, and he's usually back for lunch long before now."

"He went to look for the poachers, Marthe," Mrs. Bernard replied soothingly. "That will take him most of the day."

"For the poachers! In the forest! But he went out alone," Marthe wailed. "Why did he do that? He's known about those poachers for a long time now. He should have known better than to try to take them on by himself."

"What do you mean he's known about them for a long time?" Mrs. Bernard exclaimed. "He didn't say anything about them to me until last night."

"Well, I've known for a long time. He told me about them about a month ago," Marthe replied, a worried frown on her face. "At first he thought it was a local boy, and even after he realized it was professional, he didn't want to say anything about it to you. He thought he could handle everything without worrying anyone else. But a man of his age chasing after a whole gang all by himself, well...it's crazy. He says he can always run if he gets into any trouble. But can you imagine his doing that at his age? I've been worried sick, I'll tell you at the thought that he might meet up with those characters!"

"Why didn't he tell me about them sooner?" Mrs. Bernard asked.

"As I said, for a while he thought he could handle it, ma'am," Marthe replied. "And at first, I thought he could, too. We both suspected the blacksmith's son immediately, so he kept a close watch on him. But then the boy went off to Nevers and the poaching still went on.

"Even then," the old servant continued, "Charles didn't want to add to your worries, so he started going into the reserve at night to try to find out what was going on. It wasn't long before he realized he was up against something more serious than just a stray poacher. Such extensive operations could only be one by an organized gang."

"He should have told the game wardens as soon as he realized what was going on," Leo said.

"He did, Mister Leo, but the wardens have so much territory to cover they just can't be there all the time. One of them came over the other day and told us it's the same gang that nearly ruined the Dupont reserve, professional poachers who are well known to both the police and the game wardens. They're specialists in this kind of thing and are capable of anything. 'A mean bunch,' those were the warden's very words."

"Marthe, I'll get in touch with the chief warden right away. Don't worry about Charles, I'm sure he'll be fine." Impulsively Mrs. Bernard put her hand on Marthe's arm.

"Thank you, ma'am, I'd certainly breathe easier," Marthe said, a grateful smile on her lined face. "Now, shall I bring you your coffee in the garden?"

"Thank you, Marthe, that would be very pleasant. And, Marthe," Mrs. Bernard called as the servant turned to go, "don't worry about Charles. He knows what he's doing."

"The farmhands are probably in league with the poachers," Diane commented softly when Marthe had left the room.

"I doubt it," Leo marked calmly. "They know what would happen to them if they ever got caught. But even if they were stupid enough to be poaching, it would be to line their own pockets. They would never get involved with a gang."

"Leo is right," Mrs. Bernard remarked, nodding her head in approval. "We must think about the poachers rationally—as unemotionally as possible. Things are far too complicated without jumping to all kinds of wild conclusions."

At that moment Marthe came into the garden carrying a tray laden with porcelain demitasse cups and a delicately ornate silver coffeepot.

"Let's not talk about the poachers," Mrs. Bernard said, pouring out the coffee and passing a cup to Diane.

"Your flowers are lovely, darling," she said admiringly to her granddaughter. "How I wish I had your green thumb!"

"You should have a gardener, Diane," Leo interjected airily. "Menial labor is not for such delicate hands as yours."

"But I love gardening, Leo," Diane said, surprised at her fiancé's casual dismissal of her hobby. "Looking after the plants gives me no end of pleasure."

"Darling, you're simply saying that to hide the fact that you haven't the money for a gardener. Commendable, of course, but...."

"Money has nothing to do with it, Leo," Mrs. Bernard interrupted stiffly. "Diane's is a labor of love... not of necessity."

Leo looked up quickly at the old woman but saw no laughter in her eyes.

"Are you coming to the horse show next week, Mrs. Bernard?" he asked, hastily changing the subject.

"I doubt it, Leo. I only seem to engender problems when I leave this place," the old lady sighed, shaking her head. "I must say, I don't know how my husband did it. The estate used to run so smoothly when he was alive. Were the hands as difficult to manage back then, I wonder. Maybe they just dislike working for a woman," she concluded. "More coffee, Diane?"

"Tell Leo how you and grandfather met," Diane urged, having caught the wistful look on her grandmother's face as she referred to her late husband.

"Now that is a truly romantic story," Mrs. Bernard said, smiling. "My parents had a house just off the Bois de Boulogne, and every evening, at about the same time, I would go riding there. I had a beautiful horse— you would have loved him, Leo—which I kept in the stables, right in the Bois.

"Well, it so happened that Diane's grandfather was in Paris for a week on business, and he fell into the habit of walking in the Bois in the evenings instead of staying cooped up in his hotel room. He saw me riding on two or three occasions, and one evening he tracked down the stables in an effort to find out who I was.

"He must have given a few francs to the stable boy there, because he managed to find out both my name and address.

"Well, one morning, a dozen yellow roses were delivered to me, with a note that read 'To the beautiful equestrienne who graces the Bois de Boulogne.' And it was signed Jean-Louis Bernard.

"Naturally, I had no idea who the man was, though I think my mother suspected, on seeing the card, that I'd been keeping secret assignations with a mysterious lover!

"Anyway, the next day he sent a note asking if he could call on me. He'd sent a hotel messenger boy who'd been told to wait for my reply. And my mother very solemnly gave me permission to invite this mysterious Mr. Bernard for a glass of wine before dinner that same evening."

"Oh, grandmother, how romantic!" Diane interjected softly.

"He was a very romantic man," Mrs. Bernard agreed, nostalgically.

"Now where was I? Oh, yes. I remember being terribly nervous and shy, wondering what on earth I would say to this stranger. Of course, I wondered what he'd look like, too."

"Was it love at first sight?" Diane asked eagerly. She had heard the story many times, but it always engrossed her.

"Almost, my dear," her grandmother smiled. "When the doorbell rang, I nearly fainted with nervousness. I remember my mother coming out of her bedroom, all stiffness and primness, and saying to me, 'come along, Céline, your suitor is here.' And together we walked downstairs.

"When I saw him I was even more nervous. How handsome he was! Dark hair and mustache, and bright green eyes. He was very tanned, and I could tell by his carriage and his hands that he was probably a rider as well.

"He kissed my hand, gazed into my eyes and said, 'Miss Couture, I'm charmed. You're even more beautiful than I remembered.'" A faint blush came to Mrs. Bernard's cheek as she recounted the incident.

"We conversed easily, I remember," the old woman continued, a dreamy quality in her voice. She was obviously reliving the episode. "We talked about riding and the beauty of having a forest right in the middle of Paris.

"I was utterly charmed, and even my mother seemed to relax as she sat with us, listening raptly as he talked about Black Oaks. He talked about the stables, the farmlands, the house—all of it—with such a passion."

"Did he propose then, grandmother?"

"Oh, no, child, good heavens! He left after about an

hour, asking if he could visit again next time he was in Paris. Then he proposed!"

"A charming story, Mrs. B," Leo commented when the woman stopped speaking. "Now, I regret, I must be off. I have an appointment with a lumberman at four o'clock."

"If it's an important appointment, Leo, please don't miss it on our account," Mrs. Bernard said quickly.

"Actually, it is quite important," he replied. "However, I don't like leaving you like this, not knowing what's happening out there in the forest."

"Maybe you could come by tomorrow," the older woman suggested.

"Yes," he said as he got to his feet. "Yes, of course," he added abruptly, after a brief pause. "I'll come over tomorrow before I start work, and depending on what you've found out, we'll decide upon a definite course of action then. Are you coming to the car with me, Diane?" he asked, turning to go.

She was just about to answer when she heard the sound of footsteps coming from the path that led from the woods. The three of them waited expectantly to see who it was. In a few seconds a game warden came into view around the bend, running at full speed, carrying his hat in his hand. His face was streaming with perspiration.

"Quick, we need help," he panted breathlessly. "We found the poachers' truck hidden in a thicket along with two of their cars. Charles is watching the area, but they'll be coming back soon, and when they do, he'll need reinforcements."

"Hadn't we better wait for the police?" Leo asked quickly. "I'll go telephone them."

"We don't have time to wait, sir. They might be back any minute. We've got to get back to Charles right away if we want to catch them. We've had such a hard time finding them, and now that we have, I don't want to let them slip through our fingers. It's a real break finding them like this...and we found their cache, too—two deer strangled by one of the snares and a small fawn that is still alive. When I left, they were shooting around Clairfontaine. It will take them a few minutes to get from there to their vehicles, but we need every one of those seconds to be sure to get back in time to catch them red-handed."

"Get me your gun, Diane," Leo said quickly. "And would you telephone the police?" he added, looking over at Mrs. Bernard.

"Yes, of course," said the older woman. "And when they come, we'll go with them to show them the way."

"It's about a hundred yards past Bruno's Corner," the warden explained. "And tell the police to hurry. The sooner they get there, the better."

Diane came running back with her gun and a round of ammunition. Leo took it from her without seeming to notice her eyes, which were wide with fear.

Suddenly the whole atmosphere had changed, she saw. Leo had changed, too. He was excited—enthralled by a situation he hadn't really cared about a few minutes earlier. All at once he was looking forward expectantly to the possible outcome of their search with as much excitement as the young warden. As the two men strode off toward the forest, their eyes were glowing with the same fierce light.

"Well, it's up to us to do our part now," Mrs. Bernard said quietly, putting her hand gently on her granddaughter's arm. "Come on, dear, let's go. We haven't a minute to lose."

The women drove to the gate and waited for the police, who arrived in record time. Diane crossed over to their car and explained the situation hurriedly to the driver. After a few minute's conversation, she returned to her own vehicle, followed by a police officer.

"This policeman is coming with us," Diane informed her grandmother, "and the other two are following behind in their own car."

The policeman climbed into the backseat, and Mrs. Bernard immediately turned to speak to him.

"I'm looking forward to catching those thieving rascals and getting them off my land once and for all," she said.

"I agree with you there, ma'am. We know that bunch," the policeman replied, leaning forward. "Before they started on your place, they cleaned out old Mr. Dupont. Took almost every animal he had. He had three gamekeepers of his own and two wardens working almost full time on his property, but those poachers kept slipping right through their fingers, getting past them as if they weren't even there. Mr. Dupont was at his wits' end. Finally the wardens called us in. We got rid of the gang after a while, but only by saturating that forest with our men, night after night. The poachers finally gave up and moved on.

"I'm sure it's the same gang this time," the young officer continued. "They're well organized; after they've been around, any hunting ground is completely decimated. They're only after the hides, not the meat. Sometimes they skin the animals right on the spot and leave the bodies to rot—it's a horrible sight. They probably make a fair bit of money selling the skins, but it sure is a dirty business."

"I still wonder why Charles didn't tell us about them sooner," Diane remarked.

"Well, for a long time, he thought it was the blacksmith's son," Mrs. Bernard answered, turning around in her seat to include the policeman in their conversation.

"That kid certainly was doing a little poaching on his own, and we think his presence in the forest might have alerted the gang to the fact that there was a prolific game reserve there," the policeman commented.

"Anyway," he continued, "we should have known that he left almost too soon after the wardens started checking your forest as often as they could. When we took away his gun and hunting permit, we were glad to be rid of the little nuisance, but when we realized the gang had appeared, we knew we were up against a serious situation, even worse than the one they created at Dupont's place. With them, it's like trying to fight an epidemic of cholera. One minute you think you've got the poaching all cleared up, and the next minute it breaks out somewhere else."

After a few minutes, Diane said, "I think the best thing to do is for us to stop a little way before we get there so they won't hear us coming. If they see that police car behind us, they might panic."

No one in the car said another word for a while, and the serious nature of their mission began to dawn on Diane.

The accelerator was nearly to the floor, but when she glanced at her grandmother to see if she was nervous, Diane saw the old lady deep in thought, oblivious of the hurtling speed of the car. Soon they turned and shot down one of the forest's wide dirt roads, the road that led to Bruno's Corner.

After that everything happened very quickly.

As the car approached the designated spot, the silence of the countryside was shattered by a series of gunshots. Diane pressed down even harder on the accelerator, and the car shot forward. At that very moment, a truck drove out of a dark path in the woods.

With a sickening crash, the two vehicles collided head-on.

The policemen who had been following Diane leaped out of their own car and ran to the wreckage. Quickly but gently one of them helped Diane out of her seat, while the other tugged at Mrs. Bernard. She had lost consciousness, and her body was limp. The policeman who had been riding in the back stumbled out on his own, looking a little dazed.

Diane was perfectly calm. She surveyed the scene: in the truck—its front end smashed beyond recognition—two men were in the front seat. One was draped over the steering wheel, the other leaning against the passenger door, his head bleeding profusely. Almost disinterestedly, Diane watched a third poacher escape on a motorcycle. But neither of the policemen pursued him; they were laying her grandmother on the ground, a safe distance away from the crumpled car in which she had been riding only a few minutes ago.

"I'll radio for an ambulance, ma'am," Diane heard one of the policemen say to her.

"Oh, yes," she replied absently, "by all means." The officer gazed at her quizzically, then went off to use the radio in his car. Diane vaguely heard him speaking with one of the other policemen but could scarcely make out their words.

That night Diane was kept in the hospital for observation until she came out of shock. And Mrs. Bernard died of a fractured skull.

Chapter 4

For the next two weeks Diane felt nothing but an aching emptiness. Unable to release any of her pain by crying, she spent her time walking aimlessly around the estate, the two setters trailing after her. No culinary temptations of Marthe's could induce her to eat more than morsels of food at a time. She saw almost no one. The neighbors were asked not to call. When Leo came to visit, she turned him away. The farmhands paid their respects briefly and then kept away from the house.

All her actions were mechanical, and her mind benumbed. She took to walking in the woods, finding her only measure of respite amid the huge trees and the all-pervasive tranquillity.

During her first few such walks, the lumberjacks she passed called out greetings to her. But when she never responded with more than a wave of her hand, they soon refrained from interrupting her somnabulistic strolls. She meandered aimlessly, most of the time

thinking of nothing at all, occasionally remembering
things that she and her grandmother had done together
and then quickly repressing the recollections that were
now so painful.

Finally Diane responded to a persistent invitation
from Leo's mother to spend a day at Wildacres.

Leo collected her in the morning and drove her to his
parents' estate.

"Hello, my dear," Mrs. Marchand said. "I'm glad
you finally decided to come."

She kissed her guest lightly on both cheeks and then
put her arm around Diane's waist. "How are you feeling? You must be terribly lonely in that huge house all
by yourself."

Try as she might, Diane had never been able to warm
to Leo's mother. Her comments were always barbed, it
seemed, and nothing she said was ever without a
reason. Her face was beautiful but hard, Diane always
thought, a reflection, perhaps, of her manipulative
character.

Diane knew she saw this manipulative streak in Leo
as well, but so far she had been able to ignore it.

"I'm feeling fine, thank you," she replied crisply in
answer to Mrs. Marchand's question. "And I'm not at
all lonely—really, I'm not. The servants keep me company."

"I see," Mrs. Marchand said, coolly appraising
Diane. "Yes, of course...the servants." It was as if
Mrs. Marchand was not paying attention to what she
was saying, as if her mind was occupied by quite different thoughts.

Diane began to feel self-conscious. "It...it was kind
of you to invite me to stay with you, when grand-

mother died, Mrs. Marchand," she said, anxious to
smooth over the awkwardness between them.

"I still think that you're being a little perverse in that
respect, my sweet," Leo rejoined, a half smile on his
face.

"A change of scenery is so often beneficial," continued Mrs. Marchand. "Shall we go into the garden?
Leo, ask Jeanette to bring us some lemonade out in the
back."

Diane followed her hostess into the garden. It was
quite unlike the garden at Black Oaks, which was a
riotous profusion of color with many different blooms
scattered around the flowerbeds. Diane had always admired the garden at Wildacres but she found its formal,
stylized design too contrived for her taste.

Its hedges were cut absolutely square, and all the
flowerbeds were laid out side by side in perfect symme-
try, like colorful graves. The roses were lovely, however, and Diane remarked on them to Mrs. Marchand.

"Yes, Philippe does an excellent job, doesn't he? I
don't know what I'd do without such a good gardener.
Personally, I can't get a thing to grow. I have him take
care of even the plants in the house.

"Good servants are dreadfully hard to find, don't
you find? I'm sure your grandmother has problems...
oh, Diane, I'm so sorry," Irene Marchand interrupted
herself, embarrassed.

"Don't be sorry," Diane said, a thin smile on her
face. "It's inevitable that grandmother's name will
come up in conversations. There's nothing to be gained
by avoiding it."

"Here's Jeannette with the lemonade, mother," Leo
said, preceding the maid into the garden. "I think we

should probably be drinking wine, though; it's hot already, even if it's not eleven o'clock yet!"

"If you had your way, you'd have wine for breakfast," Mrs. Marchand said, teasing her son affectionately.

"Not a bad idea," Leo responded, laughing.

"Now tell me, dear," Mrs. Marchand said, turning to Diane. "What are your plans now?"

"Plans?" Diane echoed blankly.

"Well, I assume that you don't want to be alone much longer. . . ." the other woman began delicately.

"What choice do I have, Mrs. Marchand?"

"Well, dear, Leo and I have been talking and. . .well, why don't you get married sooner than you planned? After all, you're engaged, you've made up your mind. So what's the sense in waiting?"

"I. . .I don't think I'm ready to get married right now, Mrs. Marchand, to be quite honest with you. I think I'd make Leo quite a dismal wife."

"Perhaps you need Leo to take your mind off your bereavement. Have you considered that?"

"Well. . ." Diane said hesitantly. How could she tell Mrs. Marchand that somewhere in the back of her mind there still existed a reservation about marrying Leo? She loved him, yes, but there was something—some spark—missing. Had they known each other too long and began to take the idea of marriage—and each other—for granted, or was the problem something deeper?

Surely, Diane felt, a true, enduring love ought to be a love without reservation, a total giving. And try though she might to change it, there was a part of her somewhere that Leo couldn't get through to, a part of her he couldn't touch.

Diane suddenly noticed both Leo and his mother looking at her expectantly. "I really think I'd just as soon keep the wedding date in September, if you don't mind," she finally said.

"Of course, my dear, whatever you wish," Mrs. Marchand said gently. Had Diane been looking at mother and son rather than at her own hands, she would have seen an odd, almost belligerent look exchanged between them.

The subject of the forthcoming marriage was dropped, and the three of them went into lunch, conversing desultorily on very general topics. Diane murmured her praises of the new interior decoration in the living room, and Leo talked enthusiastically about the upcoming horse show.

When he finally brought her back to Black Oaks, Diane was exhausted from the incessant chatter and fled gratefully to the silent haven of her bedroom.

WITHIN A FEW DAYS of her visit to Wildacres, Diane's emotions began to come back. Her return to being able to feel anything was very gradual at first, like the recovery of someone who was temporarily paralyzed. Then, one evening after dinner, she suddenly broke down and cried. She wept uncontrollably, agonized sobs shaking her slim body.

It was a release at last. Gratefully accepting the cup of tea Marthe gave her, she sat in the living room, absently petting the dogs, and waited until the last of her tears subsided.

She forced herself to consider her situation. She was alone, and she had to run the entire estate by herself. Her grandmother had kept her informed on a daily basis of all important matters pertaining to the estate, but Diane had never been other than indirectly involved in the running of the place, much less the making of plans or decisions. She had never so much as had to give orders.

Mrs. Bernard had handled everything: the house, the farm, the lumber business. She had had an acute understanding of the workings of each enterprise, and everything had run smoothly under her most competent management. Diane was miserably aware of the weight of all the decisions she would have to make now that her grandmother was gone.

THE NEXT MORNING Diane got up just as dawn was breaking over the forest, casting its shimmering pink light over the trees and tinting them with a full spectrum of colors. The air was full of birds singing, and through the leaves that hung before her little, square window like a thin, green curtain, she could see little glimpses of the sparkling waters of the pond flashing and dancing with gold and silver lights from the pale morning sun. It was a glorious morning. The frogs were croaking lazily, joining their hoarse, raucous voices to those of the ducks that were floating slowly among the bulrushes in the pond. *The forest in summer sounds like a love song*, she thought, *an orchestra of sounds, all different yet blending to make up a glorious symphony.*

Even though she was still deeply grieved and felt keenly the loss of her grandmother, Diane couldn't help be affected by the joyous sounds of early summer and allowed them to ease her aching heart.

When she had dressed, she went downstairs to the

dining room, just as her grandmother had done every morning of her married life. Germaine, Marthe and Charles were waiting for her. Her place had been set at the long wooden table, and as she took her seat, Marthe hurried to serve her mistress breakfast. Charles stood quietly off to one side, turning his hat awkwardly over and over in his hand, obviously waiting for the right moment to speak his mind.

"Did you sleep well, Miss Diane?" Marthe asked solicitously.

"Yes thanks, Marthe," Diane replied.

"Do you have any orders for me, Miss Diane?" Charles asked.

"I think you should go to the tree felling at Courelle," she replied pensively. "I haven't time today. The lawyer said he was coming to see me this morning, but he didn't say exactly when. So I'll have to stay near the house until he comes."

"The lawyer—" Marthe began, then stopped short as if she was afraid to go on.

All three servants looked at Diane, worried expressions on their faces.

"Did you say the lawyer is coming here, Miss Diane?" Germaine blurted, visibly mustering up all her courage, "You're not going to sell Black Oaks, are you?"

Diane sensed immediately the apprehension that had prompted the woman's question and realized that the servants must have discussed among themselves the possibility of her selling the estate.

She hurried to reassure them. "Please don't concern yourselves," she said warmly, addressing all three of them. "I'm not going to sell a thing—that's not why the lawyer is coming. He's bringing over some papers and deeds for me to sign, that's all."

The three servants relaxed visibly, the apprehensive looks on their faces melting into smiles of relief.

"We were afraid you might want to sell the place because you think it's too much for you to run all by yourself," Marthe said almost guiltily.

As Diane sat there at the table looking at these kindly faces, she felt a surge of affection for the old family retainers standing before her. They'd been at Black Oaks as long as she could remember. "You're here with me. That's all I need," she said softly, looking at them fondly. "I'll be fine with all of you to help me."

"Well, as far as we're concerned," Marthe began, wiping away a tear that had crept down her wrinkled old cheeks, "you know you can count on us for anything you need, Miss Diane."

"I know," she said simply, "and I'm grateful."

"Gerardy is supposed to be coming over here this morning, isn't he?" Diane asked, looking over at Charles.

The old man nodded slowly. "Maybe it would be better if I went over to his house and got him," he suggested, his mouth drawn into a thin, tight line. "That way we would be sure he got here and received his orders for the day."

While she waited in the study for Gerardy to arrive, Diane looked over the notes her grandmother had left behind and those Charles had added. She had died just as the harvest was beginning. It appeared that Gerardy had managed to get about half the fields in, but that left half to go and the harvest season was almost at an end.

There was a great deal of work to be done in a very short time, she reflected.

Suddenly a loud knock at the door interrupted her thoughts. Almost immediately Gerardy strode in, a battered old hat jammed on the back of his head.

"Do you have any special orders for me today?" he asked arrogantly, as he strolled casually over to the table where Diane was sitting.

"Good morning, Gerardy," she replied calmly. "No, I haven't anything special to tell you today. I expect you're getting on with the harvest as quickly as you can."

Gerardy made no answer beyond a defiant stare, so Diane took an inconspicuous breath and continued. "However, I do want you to know I intend to go on just as my grandmother did, and I expect you to obey my wishes just as you did hers. So, every morning, you will come here to the house as usual and tell me everything that has been done on the farm the preceding day. We'll discuss how the work is going and see that both our interests are being served."

The man's ruddy complexion turned a deeper shade of red. "Mrs. Bernard knew the business well and understood what she was talking about," he muttered. "She didn't waste time shooting the breeze."

"I know the business very well, too," Diane replied calmly. "And I don't intend to waste time arguing with you as if we were business competitors. I am your employer, but we both know that we're truly co-workers in this enterprise, and that's the way I would like to approach things. I think that will serve both our interests very well. Don't you agree?"

Gerardy simply stared. Diane took another deep

breath and continued in a brisk voice, "Now, what work have you planned for your crews this morning?"

"There's a man missing this morning," the overseer replied brusquely. "I wanted to harvest the hay, but we need four men for that and I only have three."

"What's the matter? Is he sick?"

"One of the horses stepped on his foot. He's been off work for three days now. I'll have to find someone else to replace him. As a matter of fact, I should get going on that right now." He turned toward the door and began to stride to it.

"Just a minute," Diane said quickly. "I see from my grandmother's books she was planning to sell the Holstein yearling. Have you done that yet?"

The man stalled for a moment, a shifty look in his eyes. "Yes, it's sold," he replied roughly. "But we lost money on the deal. The breeder wouldn't come close to the amount we should have received."

"Gerardy," she began, getting slowly to her feet, "you know my grandmother always insisted on being present at all business transactions. Why wasn't I informed?"

"Oh, what the hell could you have done?" he exclaimed, dismissing her words with an indifferent gesture.

In that one moment, Diane felt all his contempt hit her.

"Gerardy I think you should remember that I am the mistress of Black Oaks now," she said quietly.

"Yeah, but I'm still the one who runs the farm," he replied as he turned to go. "I've got a contract that's good until the end of the year. And there ain't nothing you can do about that. If you try, I'll see you in court.

And who the hell do you think is going to run this outfit if I don't? You sure can't."

As he reached the door, he turned and shot her a nasty glance. "Two of the sheep are limping," he snapped. "And that new sow ate three of her piglets. What are you going to do about that, eh?" he asked harshly as he left the study.

Diane listened to him walk out the kitchen door and bang it closed. His arrogant laughter echoed behind him.

Chapter 5

Diane sat down again when the overseer had left. Her knees were shaking from her first direct encounter with Gerardy's rudeness and insolence.

Mrs. Bernard had frequently admitted to Diane her regret that Gerardy had been appointed overseer of all the farmland. The old lady had long suspected that he winked at a good deal of pilfering, perhaps even shared in it, but she had been thwarted every time she'd tried to prove the man's guilt. And, as she had explained to Diane, if she attempted to break his contract without absolute proof, he was the type to drag her through an unpleasant and expensive court battle. Besides, he was a good worker when he chose, and it was because there was always a shortage of competent farm overseers, Diane knew, that her grandmother had been induced to keep him on year after year.

Suddenly Diane felt terribly lonely and vulnerable. *I'm so inexperienced*, she thought wearily. *What I real-*

ly need is a manager. She resolved to talk to Mr. Garnier about it when he came.

However, her talk with her lawyer, which lasted most of the morning, wasn't very reassuring. The lumber wasn't selling very well, and for the past two seasons the revenues from the farm had not been enough to cover the operating expenses. Mrs. Bernard's personal fortune had been almost exhausted to cover the losses; after death duties were paid, the amount remaining would be negligible.

"The long-range picture isn't bad," the lawyer explained. "The land is fertile, and the timber reserves have enormous potential value. With better luck with the weather and an upswing in general business conditions—which is sure to come some day—this estate will show a good profit again. But while your grandmother was waiting for that, it was only her acute business sense that was keeping the farm and the lumber business going," Mr. Garnier commented.

"I can carry on in her place, I know I can," Diane insisted. "But I need a manager for a few months . . . just until I can become more familiar with the working of the farm. Someone who could deal with Gerardy—and help with the poachers."

"You just haven't got that kind of money, my dear. I told you that there's very little cash left. As I said, it was only your grandmother's astute business sense that has been keeping Black Oaks going. The cash flow problem is critical, and regrettably there just isn't the money to pay a manager. You're going to have enough trouble meeting your payroll and tax installment at the end of the month.

"Now, my dear," he continued, "what does Leo Marchand have to say about all this?"

"Leo?" she echoed. "Why, he's going to help me of course. He promised he would. It will be wonderful to have him here. A man of his intelligence and vitality will automatically command respect and make things so much easier for me."

"In that case," the lawyer said, "you'll probably be able to do without a manager. No doubt Mr. Marchand will give you all the help he can."

"I really hate to ask him right now," Diane murmured, as though to herself. "Leo is quite involved with his horses right now, so. . . ."

"He's getting into an expensive business," the lawyer sighed. "You must advise him to be prudent in this new venture of his. . . ."

"Yes. . . well. . . I'm sure he'll do what he thinks is best," Diane said quickly, trying to defend Leo against any disapproving comments the lawyer might make.

"Of course, my dear, of course he will," the lawyer replied soothingly. "Well, give Mr. Marchand my regards when you see him. I must be off now." And with a brief nod, he took his leave.

The trouble with the Mr. Garniers of this world, Diane muttered to herself, was that they were too familiar. *He had no business saying that Leo's horses were too expensive. How would he know, anyway?*

But though she was unwilling to admit it, the same thought had occurred to Diane. The day of her grandmother's death, she remembered, when Leo had been at Black Oaks for lunch, he'd admitted that his father had reduced his allowance. And she'd immediately thought to herself that he'd recently bought a racehorse, hired a part-time trainer and consulted an expensive veterinarian on numerous occasions. Where was the money coming from, she wondered then, and the thought recurred to her now.

Diane knew that Mr. Garnier was the Marchands' lawyer as well as her own—in fact, he was an old classmate of Mr. Marchand's—and she was curious as to just how much Leo had told him of his plans. Not that it mattered one iota, she thought with a shrug.

After lunch, Diane buried herself in her grandmother's account books. She wanted to rise to the challenge of the task that lay ahead. When she'd told Gerardy that she knew the business as well as her grandmother, she hadn't been telling the truth—at least not entirely—and he had probably guessed it.

She decided to concentrate her time entirely on the farm and the lumber business and make them work. If she put all her energy into these ventures, she knew she could ultimately make them profitable. So far, this season's weather had been good. Mr. Garnier had reassured her that the forest could be very valuable, and that her fields were the best farm land in that part of the country. Her grandmother had been quite correct in her estimate that what was needed now was a supreme effort to keep things running until business conditions improved.

Armed with this information, Diane decided to do everything in her power to continue her grandmother's strategy and eventually make her estate a success. She would let nothing stand in her way.

When Leo arrived later that afternoon, he found Diane sitting at the desk in the study, surrounded by account books from which she was taking copious notes.

"What are you doing, darling?" he asked, a puzzled

look on his face. "Why are you working like this? Your grandmother has just died, and here you are with your nose to the grindstone already. Don't you think you should rest and give yourself a chance to heal?"

"Oh, Leo, I'm so glad to see you. I need your help," she sighed. "I know the lumber business fairly well, but it's the farm I'm worried about. I've already had a run-in with Gerardy and—"

"And you'll have a lot more, too," he interrupted. "You haven't seen the last of that fellow."

"I must say you aren't very encouraging," she said, looking up at him. "I know I'm going to have trouble with him—and the other men. I was hoping you could give me some advice."

Diane rose from her chair in front of the desk and walked toward Leo. "Will you please help me?" she asked softly.

Without a word, he pulled her to him and held her close. "Oh darling, you know I want to help you all I can. I can't bear to see you tackling this huge estate all by yourself. The only thing is, my love, I can't help right away. My horses . . . ."

"Yes, yes, of course. I understand," she whispered. "I know how important the horses are to you." Diane pulled away from Leo's embrace and sat down again on the desk chair with a weary sigh.

Leo moved beside the desk and looked down at Diane. His strong tanned body, set off by leather boots and a tweed hacking jacket, cut a very virile, attractive figure, and the effect was not lost on Diane.

He gazed at her for a full minute without speaking, and Diane thought for a fleeting second that she saw a look of cold aloofness dart across his features. But in less than a second the look had disappeared, and his face expressed concern and solicitude.

Diane brushed her hand over her eyes and pushed her hair off her face. *He looked almost as if he couldn't care less*, she thought. *But he must, he promised grandmother he'd help me, and after all, the place will be his, too, once we're married. . . .*

"You look completely worn out, darling," Leo said, breaking into her thoughts. "Put Charles in charge for a while. He knows the ropes."

"Oh, Leo," Diane replied, frowning. "That's absurd. He's very faithful and willing, but he has no experience or training in management or business. Besides, he's too old."

"Well, what are you going to do then?" Leo asked, a hint of exasperation in his voice. "It will be at least a week or two before I have any time to help you and heaven only knows what murder Gerardy and his bunch will have gotten away with by then."

"I'll manage, Leo," Diane said resolutely, "with or without your help."

"Brave words, darling, brave words. I don't dispute for a minute, my sweet, that you have a fine—and beautiful—head on your shoulders. But Black Oaks is a vast estate, and you're young and inexperienced. Think again about Charles. Unless, of course. . . . No, that's out of the question."

Diane didn't ask Leo what he had been about to say. She was looking up at him as if she were seeing him for the first time.

He wasn't encouraging her at all, she thought in amazement. All he could talk about was her problems, and he never spoke in terms of "our." He was making it quite clear that he expected her to handle all this by herself, that he wouldn't be involved at all. Oh, he'd made all the right noises at the beginning, but it was dawning on Diane that he really had no intention of assisting her—ever. His horses, it was becoming quite obvious, took precedence over Black Oaks—and his fiancée.

Diane felt a sharp pain in her chest, and once again she felt very much alone. She turned away from Leo, hoping to hide the hurt she knew must be reflected in her eyes.

"Don't be upset, darling," he said. "I'm just telling you the way things really are. You know I'm only thinking of your interests. Perhaps you should even consider...."

He stopped talking abruptly, and Diane turned back to stare at him. "Just what is it you want me to consider?" she asked.

"I'll tell you later," he replied evasively. "We'll talk about all this again, not now. Right now, I've got to go."

"But Leo," Diane said in surprise. "You just got here! Why do you have to leave so suddenly?"

"I was going to ask you if... you wanted to go out for a drive," Leo said hesitantly, as if he had been about to say something but had changed his mind and hastily substituting something else. "But you seem preoccupied with your work."

"It can wait, Leo. It's nearly dinnertime, so perhaps we'd better not go out, but would you like a drink? And you're more than welcome if you'd like to stay for dinner."

"No thanks, my sweet, I'll say no to dinner, but I'd love a glass of wine."

Diane noticed that Leo seemed ill at ease as he followed her into the living room.

"Leo," she asked, after Germaine had brought in the wine, "was there some particular reason you came over today? You seem to have something on your mind."

"Simply your welfare, my sweet," he replied easily. "Nothing more than that, I assure you."

But Diane wasn't convinced. There was something in Leo's expression that made her think that he had intended to speak to her about something. She wondered what had changed his mind.

They talked about horses and riding and vets' bills, both of them carefully avoiding the subject of the management of Black Oaks.

Germaine summoned Diane to dinner a little while later, and Leo jumped up as if grateful for the opportunity to leave.

"Goodbye, darling. Look after yourself," he said, brushing his lips lightly across hers.

He strode across the room and, without a backward glance, opened the door and walked out.

Chapter 6

Three days later, Diane decided to take a short respite from her labors and go riding for the first time since her grandmother had died. The day had dawned clear and fine, and as she pulled on her jodhpurs and riding boots, she felt a childish excitement at the thought of galloping through the fallow fields at the end of the estate. Her grandfather, himself a keen horseman, had always kept several open acres unplanted for meadows, filled only with clover and masses of daisies, not unlike an English common. A horse could canter or gallop at will on those fields, and after looking at nothing but ledgers for several days, Diane felt an hour or so of riding would be just the break she needed.

"A lovely day for a ride, Miss Diane," Germaine commented conversationally, as Diane sat down to breakfast.

"Mmm, I can hardly wait," Diane said, sipping at a steaming cup of coffee.

"Would you like Charles to drive you down to the stable?"

"No, thanks, Germaine. I'm sure he's busy with other things. Is Marthe going into the village today?" The maid nodded. "Would you ask her to get some peaches and plums? They should be in the market by now."

"I'll mention it to her, miss. Anything else?"

"No, thanks. See you later; I'll be back for lunch."

The mare that Diane had been given as a birthday present when she was sixteen trotted eagerly toward her as soon as the stable door was opened. It neighed excitedly with the spirit of a much younger horse, nostrils flared to the fragrant air, as Diane put on its bridle and saddle.

"Come on, old girl," Diane said, as she led the mare outside. "You and I are going to gallop our cares away." And with a nimble practiced movement, she sprang into the saddle. She held the horse at a walk out to the field, then with a slight pressure of her thighs against the horse's side, she urged it to a trot. With another nudge, the mare began to canter.

It was beautiful day, the early morning clarity having given way to a muted softness that signaled the makings of a very hot day. Diane threw her head back, laughing with pleasure—with a joy that defied being deflated by worries and cares. This morning she was going to enjoy the beauty of her inheritance, not fret about its financial liability.

After a few minutes, Diane galloped flat out, then, as the horse began to tire, she reined it back to a canter, a trot, then finally a walk. They were some distance from the stable now, near a road that bordered the edge of the forest.

As the horse walked slowly along the grass beside the road, Diane noticed two teenage boys walking quickly out of the forest and down the road toward the farm. Her curiosity was aroused by the two strangers, and she made a mental note to find out where they came from and what they were doing on Black Oaks property. They didn't look familiar, though Diane was sure she knew most of the farmers' children. Perhaps they were visiting cousins.

But when she returned to the stables some time later, tired but exhilarated by her ride, she had completely forgotten about them.

THAT EVENING, AS USUAL, Charles came to report to Diane. She hadn't seen Gerardy for three days, not since the morning she had told him she wanted him to come every day, the way he had when her grandmother was alive. Diane knew it was a deliberate move on his part to show her he had no intention of acknowledging her as the new mistress of Black Oaks, but she felt it wise to avoid a direct confrontation with him at this time. Work was getting done, and she needed his expertise too badly to risk a showdown.

Charles, however behaved very differently. Every evening the old man dropped by, and Diane took advantage of the opportunity to discuss as many business matters as possible. She knew he shared her concerns and was trying his best to ease the burden of responsibility and solve as many of her problems as he could. However, he always told her exactly what was going on and spared her none of the painful details.

Tonight he reported, "The wind was so strong last night it tore off part of the south barn roof. I went to get Gerardy, but his wife said he wasn't home, so I took the responsibility of getting repairs started right away to avoid a complete disaster. Incidentally, when I was checking the livestock, instead of seventeen lambs in the barn, I found only thirteen. Did Gerardy talk to you about that, Miss Diane?"

"No, he didn't. He hasn't even been here for three days. He must have sold them."

"I wouldn't be at all surprised," Charles replied, nodding his head slowly.

Aside from all that, he continued, the work was going well. "The hay's all cut now, and we're just hoping now the weather will hold so we can gather the rest of it in before the rain comes. There's the making of quite a storm out there. But it will be a good harvest, Miss Diane, I'm sure of it."

"Do you know if Gerardy has enough men?"

"He's got four working on the hay, miss. I saw them stacking it when I was making my rounds. He wasn't there though. He likes to play boss," he added, laughing slightly, "but he doesn't do much of the actual work, that one."

THE NEXT MORNING, Germaine greeted Diane at the bottom of the stairs, her face red with anger. "Have you seen what's happened, miss?" she asked, her eyes flashing behind her glasses. "Those geraniums you spent so much time on are all trampled down. When I went out this morning, the ducks from the pond had gotten into the garden and were pecking away and trampling all over them. It was no accident their getting in, Gerardy's son did it on purpose. Marthe says she saw him fooling around out there yesterday evening, and today when we went out to shoo the ducks out, we found that the little gate had been held open by a rock so the wind wouldn't blow it shut."

Diane ran into the dining room and looked out across the veranda at the broken flowers. Just then, Marthe walked in.

"I hope you'll give Gerardy what for, miss," she said indignantly. "Those people are a bad lot, and he does nothing to control his own children. My word, I can't believe even a boy could do such a vicious thing. I remember when that family first came here; they didn't have a penny to their name, and Mrs. Bernard helped them get started. Now look how they repay her kindness."

"People have short memories," Diane said bitterly. "But, unfortunately, it probably won't do much good to confront them about this."

"But you can't let it go by without doing something," Germaine protested. "If they do, they'll think they can get away with anything they want. They'll start thinking they're running things around here, and God help us then. Look, there's Gerardy now," she said, indicating the overseer who was striding toward the house. "Doesn't he look proud of himself this morning."

The two servants slipped quietly away, leaving Diane alone with her thoughts. She had learned a great deal these last few days, she thought grimly.

When Gerardy came into the room, Diane stood waiting, pale and nervous, her hand gripping the dining room table. When he saw the icy look in her eyes, his arrogant expression softened a little.

Without wasting any time, she came straight to the

point. "Why did you let your son let the ducks into the yard? Is this your idea of a joke?"

He was taken aback by her frontal attack and seemed momentarily embarrassed and lost for a response. "They must have gotten in by themselves," he replied finally. "The gate wasn't closed properly and the wind probably—"

"And I suppose it was the wind that put the stone there to keep the gate open," she interrupted brusquely.

Realizing he had obviously neglected to remove the incriminating evidence, the overseer replied aggressively. "Well, what of it? Boys will be boys. And if the ducks find something in your garden that they like to eat, it's just as much your fault as it is his."

"That's enough," she replied coldly, looking him straight in the eye. "I don't want it to happen again— ever."

"Now, why are you here?" she continued. "Did you want to talk to me about something?"

"Yeah, I do," he replied with a contemptuous laugh. "And you're not going to like it. Four lambs have died and—"

"And instead of burying them, you took them away in your truck the night before last. I know whom you sold them to, Gerardy. And mark my words, this is going to cost you more than if you'd let them die of an illness. You can count on that."

He turned scarlet, clenched his fists and took a step toward her. "Are you calling me a thief?" he said menacingly.

"Yes I am. At first I couldn't believe you would act so blatantly. So when I heard talk of the missing lambs, I did a little checking up. You can't hide anything around here, Gerardy. It's a small community. People see things and they talk."

He heaved a sigh and glared at her. Diane looked at his eyes and wished Leo were there. Her fiancé could surely handle this man much better than she could. Gerardy was tall and powerful, and he would be more impressed by brute strength than by any rational approach she might take with him. Leo would never allow him to treat her the way he did now.

If only Leo were here now, she thought, as she stared at Gerardy's face, which was suffused with anger. However, he wasn't here, Diane thought miserably, and she would just have to do the best she could. She couldn't afford to attempt to break Gerardy's contract in midseason—much less attempt to run the place without him— but neither could she afford to let him ride roughshod. So the overseer mustn't guess how frightened she was, no matter what giving such an impression cost her.

"That's all I have to say to you today," she said coldly, trying to hide the fear in her voice. She stood motionless in front of him, returning his furious gaze with a calm, level stare.

He sighed loudly, then shrugged indifferently. "There's a storm brewing," he said finally. "If it breaks before nightfall, it will spoil the rest of the hay. But it might help something else."

With this enigmatic remark, he turned on his heels and marched out of the room.

He hadn't been gone a minute before Marthe and Germaine came back into the room, followed by the two dogs.

"Oh, Miss Diane, we were so afraid for you. We

were listening outside the door to make sure you were all right," Marthe cried. "We were ready to rush right in if we heard you cry out."

"You did well not to come in," she replied. "It would only have aggravated matters. However, I don't think he would have tried anything. He wouldn't dare."

"I'm not so sure about that," Germaine cried. "You never can tell with a ruffian like him—he's capable of anything. The dogs don't like him either. That's never a good sign when the dogs don't like somebody."

"I guess we'll just have to get used to each other," Diane said wearily. "I'm going to let him go the minute his contract expires, but until then, he's going to have to learn to toe the line. He's just going to have to accept the fact that I'm mistress here now and that he has to obey my orders."

Chapter 7

That afternoon, Diane donned her heavy-duty raincoat and waterproof boots and set off into the forest to visit the lumberjacks. The storm hadn't yet broken, but thunder rumbled in the distance and angry, turbulent storm clouds gathered ominously overhead, obliterating the sun and reflecting an eerie yellow light.

She spent about an hour talking with the men about their equipment and quarters as well as the condition of the trees, a field in which she was quite knowledgeable.

In the course of the conversation, the lumberjacks informed her they hadn't seen hide nor hair of any poachers recently. However, one of them had discovered a wild boar trap in the woods a few days earlier and had given it to Charles. They assured her, however, that there were plenty of deer left in the forest. In fact, that morning around dawn, they had seen two of them with their fawns.

"Those deer really stick together," said one of the oldest lumberjacks. "The mothers look after their babies for over a year, and a buck never strays far from the does under his protection. When it comes to loyalty, they're a whole lot better than human beings, that's for sure."

"And they're so beautiful," another man joined in. "It's a pleasure to watch them—I love working here in the forest surrounded by them. Whenever I catch a glimpse of one, I stop what I'm doing and just stand real quiet until they move off. It's too bad they have to be killed. They're so beautiful.

"Hey, looks like a bad storm coming," he changed the subject suddenly, looking up toward the sky. "The flies are getting bad and the leaves are starting to droop. I think we're in for a big one."

Diane said goodbye to the men and started back to the house, the echo of ax against wood following her almost all the way home. As she made her way through the woods, she wondered where she could get enough money to pay them their wages at the end of the month, much less to repair the bunkhouse roof they had reported as leaking badly. Maybe Leo could suggest something. . . .

And yet she felt reluctant to ask her fiancé for advice in this matter. Neither did she want to approach his father. She didn't like Mr. Marchand very much. He was a cold man, and for some reason, she found herself a little bit afraid of him. Yet he was a good lawyer and could probably advise her better than anyone else she knew. She remembered her grandmother had consulted him on various occasions and had always been more than satisfied with his advice.

She had only been ten years old when the Marchand family had bought the Wildacres property and moved into the magnificent old château. Leo had been thirteen at the time. *Fifteen years ago*, she thought. *It seems like yesterday.*

At first, the Marchands had only spent their vacations there. But when Leo had finished school, Mr. Marchand had sold his practice in Paris, and much to the delight of the two young people, who saw each other every chance they got, the whole family had moved to Wildacres permanently. Diane had often wondered what kind of life Mrs. Marchand, that chic, elegant woman, found out in the middle of nowhere, with so few neighbors. But she never seemed to complain, and if she missed her life in Paris, she never mentioned it to anyone.

Mr. Marchand had first wanted his son to follow him into the law, then decided he should go into the lumber business. But Leo had resisted both ideas right from the start. *If only he had followed his father's advice*, she thought. *He would be such a help to me now when I need it so badly.* She remembered the violent arguments between father and son that Leo had always described to her in minute detail. Mrs. Marchand, however, had always taken her son's side and backed him all the way in whatever he wanted to do. It was as if she couldn't refuse him anything.

As Diane walked along, pondering her memories, suddenly she realized the air had become unbearably hot, and she longed to reach the cool, dim rooms of Black Oaks.

As she neared the edge of the forest, she saw Leo standing near the pond. When he saw her, he waved cheerily and ran toward her.

"Darling!" he cried, throwing his arms around her.

"I'm so glad to see you. It seems like an eternity since we've been together, though I know it's only been four days. Sorry I haven't been over sooner, but Golden Boy had an accident. He fell against the side of the trailer and hurt his shoulder. I had to wait until the wound healed before I felt I could leave him. Aside from that, everything is perfect. I was very satisfied with his performance this morning, when I put him through the jump."

Catching sight of Diane's face, Leo smiled in an even more determined way. "How are you, darling? How have things been going here?"

"Not as well as I would like," she replied flatly.

"You don't sound very happy. Are you keeping something from me? Are you sure everything is all right?" he asked, looking at her solicitously.

"Everything is fine. Really."

He took her arm and fell into step beside her. "You had me worried there for a minute," he said tenderly. "But I still don't like that look on your face, Diane. You seem tired, worn out, worried. You can't hide anything from me, darling. You're still having problems with Gerardy, aren't you?"

"How did you know?"

"I went into the house to look for you and bumped into Germaine. She told me what happened this morning," he explained, laughing softly. "I've never seen her so upset. When I saw the geraniums, I asked her what had happened, and she told me everything.

"You know, I'm really concerned about all this," Leo added more seriously. "I don't like the thought of you having to deal with a man like that—it worries me. I think he's capable of anything...I don't trust him one bit. Why, I wouldn't be surprised if he even tried to...."

"Now don't go overboard, Leo. He's not going to kill me, you know," Diane protested. "When his contract's up, I'm going to give him his walking papers. I'll do it all according to the specifications of the contract and will send all the necessary registered letters and everything. Then I'll be in complete charge of the place and will be able to hire better workers. I'll be rid of those lazy farmhand friends of his once and for all and will be able to start fresh."

"But during the time that's still left on his contract, what is going to happen to the farm?" asked Leo. "Do you think he'll just quietly work off his time and then go? Don't be naive, Diane. If he and his buddies know they're going to be fired, they'll steal everything they can get their hands on. Why shouldn't they? You don't think they're just going to hang around for the rest of the year doing good work and then leave, do you? Why, they'll steal you blind. And once they're gone, who are you going to hire in their place?"

"I'm going to hire some good, honest, hard-working people who can live and work together in harmony," Diane said resolutely.

"Oh, come on, Diane. Be realistic."

"And I'm counting on you to help me with all this, Leo. In fact, I was hoping you could be—"

"Your fiancé who adores you and wants only your happiness?" he interrupted. "Well, that's exactly what I am. Nothing more, nothing less.

"Anyway, Germaine also said that Gerardy hadn't come over to see you for a few days. When she told me you'd gone out to the forest, I was worried you were on your way to the farm to talk to him. You must take care, my sweet."

Diane chose to ignore Leo's faintly patronizing remark and suggested instead that they have a cool drink inside the house. The humidity outside was becoming oppressive, and Diane could sense that her temper was getting short.

Inside the living room the air was cool and fresh. Leo sat down near the table in a big, old-fashioned armchair. With a sigh of relief, he stretched out his long legs on the gray flagstones and relaxed.

"What about the hay, darling? Is it all harvested yet?" he asked as Diane came in with two icy glasses.

"Not quite, unfortunately. And I'm afraid the storm is going—"

Her words were cut short by an ear-splitting crack of thunder that shook the windowpanes.

"Here it comes," Leo commented, gazing out the window. "Too bad it couldn't have held off a little longer. Is there still a lot of hay left to come in?"

"There are still several fields left."

"If the storm doesn't last long, you might still be all right. But if the rain lasts a week, well. . . ."

Diane placed her glass gently on the table and looked over at him, her dark eyes flashing. "Why are you always trying to discourage me?" she asked with deceptive calm.

"Discourage you?" he exclaimed. "I'm not trying to do that, Diane. I just want to make you understand how difficult farming is and how hard it is to make a go of it. It's a precarious business. You never know what's going to happen from one day to the next. And the weather is always a very real problem. A hail storm, heavy rains, a drought. Any one of these and your crops are lost...wiped out. And there you are with nothing to show for all the hard work and money you poured into it. I just can't see you spending your whole life struggling uselessly against the elements for so little return."

"All right then," she said, nearing the end of her patience. "Tell me what you think I should do."

"If you listen to me without going off the deep end, I'll tell you what I think would be best," he said matter-of-factly.

"I'm not the type of person who goes off the deep end at the drop of a hat, Leo. You know that. So, go on, tell me. I'm listening."

In the distance, a long roll of thunder could be heard. "I know you'll agree with me," he began, avoiding her eyes. "Look, Diane. We love each other, and nothing in the world is going to keep us apart."

Leo paused, looked hard at Diane and began again, speaking very softly and deliberately. "Now, you know that when two people get married, the wife throws in her lot with her husband. His life becomes her life. 'Whither thou goest,' and all that. Well, it just so happens that the life I want to lead is completely different from yours right now. I can't give up my work, Diane, I love it too much. Besides, I've already invested a great deal of money in it. Wildacres is the perfect place to breed horses—I couldn't possibly do it here at Black Oaks. Now, are we going to have to live apart half the time just because you won't give up this crazy scheme of yours?"

Diane still didn't know what he was leading up to, but she was beginning to feel frightened, as if some unknown danger were lying in wait for her. She sat quietly watching him, her eyes riveted on his handsome face, deeply tanned from the sun and wind. "Go on," she said quietly.

"Well," he said, taking a deep breath. "If you want to be sensible about all this, instead of living a life weighed down by impossible responsibilities that will end up crushing you, you could always sell. . . ."

"Sell!" she gasped.

"Please, darling," Leo said soothingly. "Don't get so excited. All you have to do is to choose between a life filled with worry and hardship and a life of luxury. Now, that's not such a difficult choice, is it? Just think, Diane. We could do all kinds of things together. Go to horse shows, meet interesting people—all kinds of wonderful things. Travel, maybe. This estate would fetch an enormous amount of money—we could have a great life together.

"Right now all you have is worries and responsibilities," he continued relentlessly. "Without sounding like the voice of doom, I've got to tell you I don't think things are going to get any better. But if you were to sell, not only would you not have a care in the world but you'd be an extremely rich woman. . . ."

Diane heard him talking to her as if through a dense fog. She'd never even considered selling Black Oaks. She'd been ready to do everything in her power to struggle to make things work out for the family estate and had been ready to listen to any suggestion Leo had. But she hadn't been ready for this. Not in a thousand years had she ever thought it would come to this.

Taking Diane's silence as an indication that she was considering his proposal, Leo pressed his advantage.

"Oh, Diane, you know yourself, and it's true. You deserve the best—all the good things—everything that is fine and worthwhile. I know my idea must come as a shock to you, but once you've had time to think it over, I'm sure you'll see I'm right."

He got to his feet and leaned over to kiss her forehead. "The storm is going to break any minute now. I can't stay much longer. Think about what I've just said, darling, and listen to both your head and your heart. I'm sure they won't steer you wrong. If you're honest with yourself you'll see that what I'm suggesting is the only sane course to take at this point."

After he had gone, the fragrance of his English tobacco still lingered in the room. Diane sat without moving, almost in a trance, overwhelmed by his suggestion. She felt as if someone had hit her and left her gasping for breath. She didn't care about being rich, about living in the lap of luxury. How could she possibly enjoy any money she received from losing her integrity and reneging on her love for Black Oaks? No. If she gave in and sold her home, she knew she would be swamped by guilt and remorse for the rest of her life.

At the dinner table that evening, Diane sat lost in thought, quietly picking away at her food while Marthe and Germaine, looking more and more worried by her obvious distress, served the meal in silence.

She didn't know what to do. All she wanted at this point was peace and quiet. Yet simultaneously she felt more and more overwhelmed by a loneliness that until now had been totally unfamiliar to her.

Long after the servants had closed up the house for the night, Diane sat at the dining-room table, staring off into space. It was the time of the night when the old house creaked from the heat of the day and every little sound seemed amplified in the silence. Between the great booms of thunder and the gusts of wind that rattled the windows, she could hear all the little noises of the house.

Suddenly she heard three sharp knocks at the dining-room window. Mystified, but, for some reason, not at all frightened, Diane walked the length of the dining room and opened the shutters.

Chapter 8

Diane saw a tall man in dark corduroys and a cotton shirt standing outside the window. She pointed to the front door and, securing the shutter on the window, went out to the hall to let him in.

Just then a streak of lightning was followed by a crash of thunder, and all the lights went out.

"I hope I didn't frighten you when I knocked," the stranger said, easing a knapsack off his back.

"No, you didn't frighten me, oddly enough," Diane replied, standing to one side as he removed his shoes. To herself, she wryly admitted that his arrival was, in fact, a welcome distraction from her painful thoughts.

"You're very brave," he said, laughing softly.

Suddenly the electricity came back on.

The first thing she noticed about the stranger was his smile. He was a handsome man, strong and virile, his face full of life and laughter. The dogs hadn't even barked at him, she realized. After smelling his knapsack and sniffing at him for a few moments, they had lain down again quietly.

The stranger stayed standing where he was by the door. "Are you alone?" he asked.

Diane nodded.

"But you don't live here alone, do you?"

"Well, there are three live-in servants."

He took a couple of steps forward and Diane felt her cheeks flush under the burning scrutiny of his clear, gray eyes. As she stood before him, the light of the crystal chandelier caught the gold and silver highlights in her hair.

"What an incredible picture you make, standing here in this wonderful old house," he said quietly. "I thought for a moment I'd stepped back in time to another age."

The stranger stopped talking but continued to gaze intently at Diane.

Feeling self-conscious, Diane stared down at the silver bracelet she'd been twisting around her wrist while they spoke. "Please sit down," she murmured finally, leading the man into the study. "Would you like something hot to drink?"

"Thank you, if it won't be too much trouble." Nodding gratefully at her offer of coffee, he watched her as she walked out of the room toward the kitchen.

A few minutes later, Diane returned with a pot of coffee and hot milk and a plate of bread and cheese.

"I didn't know if you were hungry," she said shyly as she caught him looking at the food heaped on the plate.

"A beautiful lady in a beautiful house," he replied.

For a minute neither of them spoke. The silence was

comfortable, however. Outside, the rain lashed furiously against the shutters.

"Are you traveling far?" Diane asked at length.

"I'm not headed anywhere in particular," the stranger replied. He was sitting in an armchair, his legs stretched out in front of him. "You could say I'm on a walking tour of the area. I never make any kind of schedule, though; I just move wherever my feet take me. That explains, I'm afraid," he added after a pause, "why I have been obliged to impose on you this most inclement of evenings."

Then he asked bluntly, "Do you have any family?"

Something in his face, in the gentleness of his voice and manner, made Diane want to confide in this man. Far from taking offense at his very personal question, she almost welcomed it. Perhaps, it was a chance to share some of the problems that burdened her.

"I did until about three weeks ago. My grandmother died then."

"Oh, I'm sorry. I didn't mean to bring up any painful subjects," he said, looking at her kindly. "Your grandmother certainly left you a beautiful place here."

"Yes, she did. But she left me a hard row to hoe, too."

He said nothing but looked at her with obvious interest. "I guess she thought if she could manage here, so could you. That's quite a legacy. She must have thought a great deal of you," he said gently.

Suddenly Diane felt deeply relieved. His words were like a breath of fresh air, sweeping away all her doubts, hesitations and fears.

But why didn't Leo make her feel like this? Why couldn't he speak to her like this man?

"You mustn't be afraid of all the responsibilities and the hard work you have to do to meet them," the stranger continued. "That's what being human is all about. The easy life is for the weak or for those too stupid to see what real life has to offer."

Diane felt the blood rush to her face, and she blushed as furiously as if his words applied to her.

Who is this prophet who has come in with the night, Diane asked herself theatrically. *I think this is probably a dream. When I wake up he'll be gone.*

"Good lady," he went on, rising from his chair and bowing to her in mock seriousness. "My name is Martin Leblanc. And having enjoyed your hospitality, may I be permitted to know your name?"

"Diane...Bernard," she answered shyly, feeling herself flushing again under his steady gaze.

Well, Martin Leblanc, you're one of the most attractive men I've ever laid eyes on, Diane said to herself. *Even if you are a dream*, she added quickly.

The man gazing at her was about six feet tall with blond hair that, like hers, had been bleached by the summer sun. His skin was deeply tanned, as if he had been outdoors a great deal, but it was his eyes that arrested her. They were a clear dove gray, full of understanding as well as laughter, and they reflected his disarming smile.

"You can sleep on the sofa here in the study," Diane heard herself saying. "I'll...I'll get a blanket and a pillow for you."

As she turned to leave, she felt Martin's arms come up around her.

"Thank you, beautiful lady," he whispered as he kissed the nape of her neck. Before she had time to protest, Martin had released her and walked back to his chair.

Confused, Diane fled from the room to the linen cupboard on the second floor, taking the stairs two at a time.

When she returned with the blanket and pillow, Martin made no reference to the incident of a few minutes earlier.

"Tell me about yourself, Diane," he asked suddenly, but in a gentle voice.

"Well," Diane began, at a loss for words. What did he want to know, she wondered, and how much should she tell him? Diane was not particularly reserved by nature. Her grandmother had often said that her honesty and openness were desirable virtues.

Sitting on the edge of the sofa, her long, slim legs straight out in front of her, she started to tell Martin about her family. The words at first came falteringly, but as her self-consciousness diminished and she relaxed, she found the words tumbling out.

"My grandmother had two sons, one of whom was my father. My parents were killed in a car accident when I was about two years old, so my grandmother brought me to live with her here. I've lived here ever since I can remember; this is home."

"And your uncle, Diane?" Martin asked softly. "Can't he give you some help here?"

"Good heavens, no," Diane said with a little laugh. "Uncle George went off to the Ivory Coast about twenty years ago to make his fortune. Grandmother used to say that he fancied himself as an adventurer. Anyway, he hasn't been back since—I've never even met him."

"You must have been very close to your grandmother," Martin said.

"Yes, I was," she answered simply.

The rain was not teeming down as it had been earlier in the evening. Instead, there was a gentle, steady patter as the raindrops hit the ground and the windowsills. The sound was soothing, restful.

"What's the name of this wonderful old house?" the stranger asked Diane.

"Black Oaks."

"That's a good solid name, a dignified name. Black Oaks," he repeated slowly. "I can understand that you must be very happy here, Diane, and I'm convinced that you'll stay here all your life and continue to be happy." He paused.

"And you know, I think I could be very happy here, too," he added, almost to himself.

"Are you staying in this part of the country long?" Diane asked quickly, aware somehow that his answer would mean more to her than it should.

"I don't know," he replied, laughing softly. "It depends on a number of things. But you'll see me again, beautiful Diane. I can assure you of that."

"I'll say goodnight to you now," Diane murmured, self-consciously. "It's very late."

"Yes," Martin said, "it's time for sleep. 'Sleep that knits up the raveled sleeve of care.' Sleep well, Diane, and take up the good fight again tomorrow. I'll ge gone before you're up . . . but I'll be back."

Diane left the pillow and blanket on the sofa, then slipped upstairs. She undressed quickly and put the light out but was unable to sleep. Through the shutters she could see the moon, bright and silver in the black sky. The rain had stopped, leaving the night silent.

How compassionate and sensitive Martin was! How understanding and supportive! Diane felt as if, simply by talking to him, her troubles had become much less serious than she'd imagined them to be. And, more than ever, she resolved never to part with her beloved Black Oaks.

THE NEXT MORNING Diane woke later than usual and did an extraordinary thing for her. Instead of climbing into jeans and a shirt and going down to breakfast and then immediately to work in the study, she rang the bell by her bed for Germaine.

Germaine must have thought she was sick, Diane thought to herself, for the woman arrived speedily at her mistress's side.

"I'm feeling terribly lazy today, Germaine," Diane told the maid with a sleepy smile. "Would you indulge me this once by bringing me coffee and croissants up here? Oh, and the newspaper and mail, as well, if you don't mind. Thank you."

"Well, Miss Diane, you certainly look well enough. Up late last night, were you?" the older woman asked maternally as she opened the shutters to a sparkling beautiful day.

"Yes, Germaine...it was strange," Diane murmured.

"Well, you'll do yourself no good, miss, staying up till all hours."

Diane said nothing. She had a faraway look in her eyes and was so preoccupied by her own thoughts that she didn't even notice Germaine leave the room.

Only when the servant returned with a tray of steaming coffee and rolls and set it in front of Diane did she come out of her reverie.

How will I know if it was all a dream, Diane asked herself. *What proof do I have that this vision was flesh and blood? Maybe it was just a result of too little sleep and an overactive imagination. But it doesn't matter, really. I feel stronger, today, more resilient. So, Martin Leblanc, I don't mind if you're not real. You gave me the help I needed.*

When Diane had dressed and taken her tray into the kitchen, Germaine called to her from the study. "What on earth were you doing last night, miss? There are two blankets and a pillow folded up on the sofa here!"

Chapter 9

So there was her proof!

"I was working on the accounts last night," Diane called back to Germaine gaily, "and I had a quick nap in the middle of the evening."

Diane suddenly was bubbling over with a cheerfulness she could scarcely contain—a joy that she hadn't felt for weeks. She was humming as she turned back into the kitchen again to discuss supplies with Marthe.

"Well, your appetite seems to have improved, miss, as well as your spirits," the cook smiled, holding up the remnants of a cheese round. "You must have been famished last night, though small wonder. You haven't been eating more than scraps for weeks."

"Yes, Marthe, I am feeling better," Diane answered cheerily. "Please don't make lunch for me today," she added, "Leo is coming over in a little while to take me to Wildacres. I'll be back this afternoon, though."

The two women talked for a little while about domestic supplies, then Diane went to the study. The

account books still gave her the same figures, but somehow the totals looked a little less grim.

An hour later she'd exchanged her jeans for a red and
white flowered sundress and was in the living room
waiting for Leo. When she heard his car drive up in
front of the house, she went out to meet him, her shoulders back, her head high.

"You're looking wonderful, darling," Leo said enthusiastically, after kissing her forcefully on the lips.
"Positively radiant. What's caused the change?"

"I'm not sure," Diane answered vaguely, unwilling to
tell Leo about the nocturnal visitor.

"Golden Boy is jumping terribly well now. He's quite
recovered from his accident. I can scarcely wait for you
to see him, my sweet. He's a real beauty."

Diane gazed at Leo's classic profile almost objectively as he spoke. *His interest in me seems so superficial
sometimes. As if he is really more interested in Golden
Boy than he is in me.* But she couldn't believe that was
true and mentally kicked herself for such a stupid
thought.

"I'd love to see Golden Boy," she answered.

There was a brief pause as Leo started the car again.
Diane looked even harder at her fiancé. "Leo, there's
something bothering you, isn't there? You have a worried look on your face."

"Well, to be honest with you, there is something on
my mind. You know, of course, that father has never
been very happy with my involvement with the horses.
Well, he came back from Paris this morning determined to thwart all my plans. He's going to cut off my
allowance. Can you imagine? His timing couldn't be
worse. I'm getting ready to take Golden Boy to some of

the major competitions. He's sure to win, too, and that would let me more than repay the money I want to borrow from father. If he'd only told me how strongly he felt a long time ago, I wouldn't have gone ahead and made all my plans. But it's too late now—I'm going ahead anyway."

"But how? Where are you going to get the money?" she asked. "He's cut off your allowance, hasn't he?"

"Not yet he hasn't. He's just threatened that he can't afford to give me anything. But mother is still on my side," he added, laughing conspiratorially.

"Can't afford?" exclaimed Diane. "But I thought your parents were quite well off!"

"They were once," he cried contemptuously. "When they bought Wildacres, everything was going well for them. But for the last six months, every time father has returned from Paris he's brought us more tales of financial woes. He doesn't go into any details though, and I must admit that suits me fine."

"But why?" she asked, her voice shaking strangely. "Surely you're old enough to share your parents' financial worries if they have any. I know my grandmother always shared everything with me."

Leo shrugged and, for a moment, seemed slightly ill at ease. "I really don't want to know about their financial troubles. Besides, father is always exaggerating. That's the way he is—he dramatizes everything. Things couldn't be as bad as he says they are."

They continued driving in silence. Leo handled the car well and skillfully managed to avoid a herd of cattle lumbering along the road and a hay wagon that appeared suddenly as they rounded a bend in the road. Diane found herself thinking that, if he put his mind to it, Leo could really take a load off her shoulders and help her a great deal at Black Oaks. That morning, as she'd waited for him to come and get her, she had wondered whether or not she should tell him about her adventure the night before. But Leo was a jealous man, and Diane didn't feel like bringing his ire upon herself.

"You're very quiet today," he remarked suddenly. "We're almost at Wildacres and we haven't talked about anything important."

Did he expect her to announce her decision about selling Black Oaks right now, she wondered. What nonsense. This wasn't the time or the place to discuss such serious matters, she decided.

"Haven't talked about anything important!" she exclaimed. "You told me you were worried about money. That's important, isn't it?"

"Oh, I don't know," he said irritably. "I suppose so."

"Let's forget all our troubles for the day, Leo," she said quickly. "It doesn't do any good to dwell on them anyway, does it? It never really gets you anywhere. Listen, I'm sure I'll find some way of working things out for myself. And once I do, I'll wonder what in heaven's name I was so worried about. So don't you worry either, Leo. Everything will turn out all right for you, too. Let's just relax and enjoy our time together, all right?"

"I'm not sure it'll be all right at all," he cried angrily. "I don't want to be weighed down with problems all the time. I'm not going to spend my whole life scraping out some miserable little existence. I want the rich happy life.

"That's the way I am, and I'm not going to change," he added as the car screeched to a halt in front of his house.

WILDACRES WAS AN IMPOSING CHATEAU, built of pink brick, with two large wings flanking the main structure. The wide front steps that spanned a moat surrounding two-thirds of the building led into a courtyard; beyond stood the outbuildings. They were much older than the château and stood in a semicircle behind it, their weathered, ivy-covered stone walls blending in with the trees. On one side were the stables, on the other, the garages, and in the center, a huge doorway surmounted by a big clock.

The imposing structure was surrounded by a beautifully landscaped garden, lush, green lawns and narrow, winding pathways bordered with rare and beautiful trees. Copper beeches and white maples stood side by side, interspersed with clusters of tall, stately pines and blue cedars. In a sheltered little spot on the grounds rose a huge, magnificently gigantic bouquet of cyclomens overlooking the rest of the garden, filling the air with its sweet, heady perfume. The lawns sloped gently down to the river that wound its way around the château and flowed between flowered banks down the garden and off toward the woods beyond.

The Wildacres estate was a rich, opulent property with very little in common with Black Oaks. No attempt was made now to use its vast acreage for farming or lumbering. When Mr. Marchand had bought the place, he had spent a great deal of money installing all the modern conveniences and had poured thousands of dollars into making the house and grounds one of the showplaces in the area. But he had made no attempt to make the land productive. It was simply a large and valuable piece of real estate.

"Look," Leo said proudly pointing toward the stables. "I could really make something out of all that."

At that moment, Mrs. Marchand appeared on the front steps. She was a startlingly beautiful woman with the same finely chiseled features and clear blue eyes as her son. The family resemblance was obvious, both in looks and character.

"There you are, you two," she said affectionately, as she came down the steps toward them. "Dear Diane, I'm so glad to see you. You've neglected us all week."

The three of them walked into the main hall, and Mrs. Marchand removed her sun hat with a graceful gesture and threw it negligently on one of the Directory chairs lining the walls.

"It's impossible for me to get away often or for more than a few hours," Diane explained. "You see, there's so much for me to do. I can't just run off and leave the place whenever I feel like it. I have responsibilities now and I want to honor them as my grandmother would have."

"Of course you do, darling," the older woman replied lightly. "But you mustn't get too carried away with all that work, you know. You're young and you're engaged," she added as she looked in the mirror and gave her hair a little pat. "You must take that into account and give yourself a chance to get some rest and have some fun, too."

"That's what I've been trying to tell her," Leo joined in. "Diane takes life much too seriously for my liking."

"Let's go into the living room, shall we?" Mrs. Marchand said graciously. "It's only natural that Diane is taking life rather seriously at the moment. After all, she's just suffered a great loss. But we're going to do our best to cheer her up and make her see that life isn't all hard work."

They had just entered the living room when Mr. Marchand came out of his study and walked directly toward Diane. Every time she saw the man, Diane felt uncomfortable and ill at ease. He was always polite and charming, but there was something about him that she didn't trust. He had a furtive air and never gazed at anyone full in the face. Instead, his eyes looked away, darting around the room.

"My dear Diane, what a pleasure to see you again," he said in his soft, sibilant voice, clasping her hand in his own cool, damp one.

"Well, have you given it to Diane yet?" he asked, looking at his son.

"No I haven't father, I was waiting for you." Leo turned to Diane. "I have a surprise for you, darling," he said, picking up a long velvet box from the mantelpiece and giving it to her. "I asked mother to bring you back this little momento from Paris. I hope you like it and will cherish it always."

They all fell silent and watched as Diane opened the little velvet box. There, lying on a white satin lining, was an exquisite pearl necklace.

"But this is much too beautiful and expensive for me," she cried. "It's stunning.... This is too much, I can't possibly...."

"The cost doesn't matter," Leo said quickly. "Do you like it? Are you happy with my present, darling? That's what really counts. Not whether or not it's too expensive."

"Like it? I adore it. But, Leo, you know I'm not used to this kind of thing. I don't live this way," she stammered as she held the necklace out before her, looking in wonder at the lustrous, perfectly matched pearls.

Leo came over to her, took the pearls and placed them around her long, slender white neck. "Maybe you don't now," he said softly, "but who knows what the future holds? In the meantime, however, I hope these pearls will help you carry your burdens more easily. They're my way of saying I love you, Diane," he whispered, as he kissed her softly on the lips.

"They're perfect on you," Mrs. Marchand said warmly. "There's no doubt about it: jewels enhance a woman's beauty, and those pearls—"

"Add nothing to Diane's beauty," Mr. Marchand interrupted. "They just reflect it. My dear, you look absolutely ravishing."

Diane felt a little awkward at being the center of this kind of attention and admiration. She wasn't accustomed to expensive jewels or expensive clothes. She wasn't in her element in this kind of world at all. Although she'd been to Wildacres innumerable times, she could never get used to the opulence and rigid formality that was always a matter of course in Leo's home.

Suddenly she found herself longing for the fresh scent of the pine trees and the pungent odors of the farm. But here she was, her feet sinking into the soft pile of rich carpets, surrounded by paintings of the great masters, standing in the middle of a vast room furnished with pieces that belonged in a museum of fine antiques. Everything was so beautiful, so refined and tasteful. And yet she couldn't help feeling a lack of history here, a lack of a past that was directly connected to the inhabitants of the house, a lack of roots and ties to the land. No, that feeling wasn't here at all—not as it was at Black Oaks. Her house was almost like an art gallery in which each succeeding generation had left a picture of itself woven into the general family tapestry.

"Did the police come around to your place this morning?" Mr. Marchand asked her after they were seated for lunch.

"No, they didn't," Diane replied with surprise. "Have the poachers come back?"

"No, it's not poachers they're after this time. It's one man—a burglar, actually. For some unknown reason, he's decided to hide out somewhere in our peaceful little community."

"Well, he could do quite well here, what with all the old estates in the area," Leo remarked. "It would be a snap, really. They're so very isolated. If he stole anything, he could be miles away before the police were anywhere near the scene."

He looked over at Diane and smiled, then burst out laughing. "What in the world is the matter with you, Diane? You look as if you'd seen a ghost."

"Well, it's no wonder," Mr. Marchand broke in heatedly. "She's all alone in that big house with only a couple of old servants. How in the world could she possibly defend herself if the burglar decided to break into Black Oaks? I wouldn't be in her shoes, not for all the tea in China."

"Oh, I'm not afraid at Black Oaks," Diane said

quickly, having regained some of her composure. "I never have been really. I've certainly got lots of problems there, but fear isn't one of them."

Diane was speaking the truth when she said she wasn't afraid. When she had heard the three knocks on the window the night before, she had opened the shutters out of sheer curiosity and a genuine concern for whoever it was caught out in the storm. She had even felt grateful that an unexpected visitor had come by and rescued her from her acute depression. But she hadn't been afraid for one minute. It hadn't even occurred to her to be afraid.

"How did this man get to the area?" she asked, looking over at Mr. Marchand.

"In a stolen car. But it broke down yesterday just before the storm," he explained. "The police found it in a ditch by the side of the road. Actually, it was not far from your place."

Surely he wasn't talking about Martin, she thought. Martin couldn't possibly be a thief. . . .

"Do they have his description?" she asked casually.

"Yes, the police gave it to me," Mr. Marchand replied. "He's a little over average height, rather distinguished looking and strong enough to carry off very heavy works of art all by himself. Apparently, he's quite the connoisseur and only steals articles that are really valuable. They say antique silver is one of his preferences."

"Diane, you're going to sleep here at Wildacres, and that's all there is to it," Mrs. Marchand cried suddenly. "I wouldn't have a moment's peace knowing you were all alone in that big house with a man like that wandering around the neighborhood."

"But I'm not afraid," she protested. "And if it came right down to it, I could defend myself with no trouble at all."

"And what if he took you unaware? How would you defend yourself then, young lady?" Leo asked scornfully.

"Well, if that happened, I would still try to defend myself. Anyway, there isn't all that much worth taking in my house."

"That's a ridiculous thing to say," Leo cried. "What about your family silver? You don't seem to realize you have some very valuable pieces, Diane."

"I'll put them somewhere safe," she replied, her eyes sparkling. "Don't worry about me, Leo. I'll defend my property and my belongings against anyone who tries to take them away from me.

"There's probably a very good chance this man won't stay in the area very long, anyway," Diane continued lightly. "He's probably long gone by now. He most likely caught a bus and, with a little luck, will be at the other end of the country by nightfall. So what's the use of getting all riled up about something that will probably never happen?"

"My dear girl," Mr. Marchand said softly. "Don't fool yourself. These rich estates are very tempting to a professional thief like this. I wouldn't be too sure he's gone."

"That gives me the shivers," Mrs. Marchand said as she rose from the table. "Let's all go into the living room for coffee. And for heaven's sake, let's change the subject."

"They haven't seen him in the immediate vicinity yet," Leo said to Diane taking her by the arm. "But the minute I hear they even suspect he's in the area, I'm coming to get you and bring you back here, whether you like it or not. I just wish I could move in with you at Black Oaks until he's caught, but I don't dare—you know how people around here would talk."

"I'm sure the farmhands would be scandalized," she said, laughing. "It would be just the chance they've been waiting for to spread all kinds of juicy gossip about us!"

After lunch, Mr. Marchand made his excuses and retired to his study. A few minutes later Leo jumped up and also excused himself. "I'll be back in a few minutes, darling," he said, dropping a quick kiss on the top of Diane's head. "I'm just going to check something in the stable."

"All this talk about that burglar has me utterly terrified," Mrs. Marchand said, after Leo had left. "I've got a horrible feeling that that man's presence here at this particular time is going to bring us all very bad luck."

"But why would you think that?" Diane asked, her eyes wide with surprise. "I don't understand what you mean, Mrs. Marchand. I can't see why you should feel so frightened. After all...."

"But dear, just think what would happen if he came to Wildacres. Leo would probably kill him. Can you see yourself marrying a murderer?" she asked anxiously.

"Well, if Leo should end up in a position where he felt he had to kill him, it would be self-defense. That's not really murder," Diane replied, praying quietly to herself her mysterious night visitor wasn't the man in question.

"Well, perhaps not. But you know how forceful Leo

is, how protective, how courageous. It would be terrible if . . . ."

Mrs. Marchand paused and inclined her head toward the hallway. "Ssh, I think I hear him coming. Let's change the subject. I don't want him to know we were talking about this," she said quickly.

When Leo walked into the room, Diane got to her feet. "I'm afraid I'm going to have to ask you to take me home now, Leo. I left word for Gerardy that I'd . . . ."

"More interested in the sharecropper than in your fiancé, eh?" Leo said teasingly.

But when Diane looked up at him, there was no laughter in his eyes.

Chapter 10

A week passed after the luncheon at Wildacres, and Diane found herself nearly overwhelmed by her mounting difficulties. Gerardy hadn't come to see her for three mornings, and after the last time he had talked with her, he had gone out and knocked down two fences she had specifically said she wanted left standing. Then he had led a work crew to cut precious saplings for the replacement from the Black Oaks gardens. The lambs continued to disappear, too. Diane understood that his actions symbolized his determination to prove his independence from her and everything she stood for, but she had no idea what to do next. She almost certainly had legal grounds for breaking his contract, but doing so would surely entail a long and expensive court battle and would leave her without an overseer at the height of the summer season. Yet to continue in this fashion meant humiliation as well as financial loss.

To add to her problems Charles reported that poachers were still plundering the forest. And the first of the month—the day on which wages and taxes must be paid—loomed ever closer.

Despite her worries, Diane decided not to tell Leo how bad the situation really was. She knew what he would say, and she just couldn't bear to hear him tell her to give up and sell Black Oaks. The love she had for this house and the land around it was like a beautiful plant whose roots became stronger with each obstacle that fell across her path.

Leo couldn't understand that about her. Why couldn't he see it? Why was it that the one person who should be helping her at a time like this was so uninterested? It was painful knowing he didn't care about something that meant so much to her. He didn't feel anything for Black Oaks, and she would have to accept his attitude.

But Leo was still very attractive to her in every other way, and came over to see her every day—unless, of course, a horse show or his training schedule interfered.

She had heard nothing more about the burglar who was supposed to be in the neighborhood, and as the days went by, and she became more and more absorbed in her work, the memory of Martin Leblanc began to fade from her memory.

One evening, Leo arrived at Black Oaks looking very agitated. When he walked into the dining room, he found that Diane had spread her account books and legal papers across the huge table and was immersed in them. The dogs were curled companionably in a corner.

"What on earth are you doing working in here, darling?" he said, chuckling.

"It seemed a convenient place to sort the papers out so I could see everything at once," she replied. She could not expect him to understand that she drew a sort of strength from working in this most traditional room of the house, a spot that seemed to lend her a little of the courage of her ancestors.

"Have you heard the news, Diane?" Leo said quickly. "Our friendly burglar is still in the area. The Richards down the road have been robbed."

"When?"

"Last night, I think. I don't know all the details. You'll hear it on the radio, I expect. I came to warn you—since you so stubbornly insist on being here on your own—to put as many valuables as possible under lock and key. I've told you before, I think, that this fellow has a penchant for antique silver, so pay particular attention to those heirloom pieces of yours."

"Does your mother know that he's still around?"

"Yes. Why?"

"Oh, I just thought she would get a morbid kick out of the whole thing."

Leo burst out laughing. As he stood there in front of her, looking so handsomely virile, she realized how attractive he could be when he wanted to be.

"Mother is in a terrible state. She gave the grounds-man a revolver and told him to shoot at the first sign of anyone breaking in. She then insisted I give her my hunting rifle so she could keep it in her bedroom and she's carrying a pistol with her night and day. She's warned all the servants and told them to take the necessary precautions. It's absolutely ridiculous the way she's put everyone at Wildacres in a panic."

"What about you, Leo? Would you really shoot the man if you caught him stealing?"

"I sure would," he replied calmly. "I would shoot him before he even got the chance to start."

Diane said nothing but sat quietly lost in thought. "And I would expect you to do the same, Diane," he continued. "Now, since you're determined to stay on here all by yourself, locked up in your little gilded cage and all wrapped up in your crazy fantasies, I want you to promise me you'll shoot anyone who tries to break in."

"I always keep my gun in my bedroom," she replied laconically, "although I certainly don't see that I'll be needing it. Why did you say I had fantasies, Leo?" she asked suddenly.

"Because you do, my sweet," he replied softly. "Thinking you can run a place this size all by yourself. What is that if not a fantasy?"

He put his finger under her chin and lifted her face to his. "Look at you. Black circles under your eyes, hollow cheeks. That's what you get for clinging to these wild daydreams of yours."

Diane stepped back and turned her head, but Leo continued as if she had not moved.

"And because of your unrealistic attitude, you've put yourself in a position where you have to be bothered with that horrid overseer day after day. You're having trouble with the farm animals. You still don't know if the rain last week ruined the hay—and who knows what will happen before it's time to harvest the later crops. You've got tax bills to pay, a payroll to meet, repairs to make to a lot of outbuildings. Now, I'm not making any judgment here. I'm just pointing out the facts."

"Fortunately, I don't live in a gilded cage," Diane said, ignoring his criticism. "That's why I love it here so much."

Leo put his arms around her and pulled her close, brushing her cheeks with his lips. "Come here, you silly, stubborn lady, and give me a kiss. These days we seem more like brother and sister than two people engaged to be married."

Diane walked over to her fiancé and allowed herself to be drawn into his arms.

"But darling, why do you think I'm being stubborn?" she asked quietly. "This is my home, you know."

"I realize that, and I realize that you're very attached to it, but it's lunacy for you to stay here on your own. You haven't the knowledge nor the experience to operate the place. To run an estate the size of Black Oaks you...."

"I need a man's help. Is that what you're saying?"

"Yes," Leo answered after the barest hesitation. "And unfortunately...I'm not your man."

The baldness of Leo's statement hit Diane like a slap. "Do you mean you're refusing to give me any help whatsoever in the running of Black Oaks?" she asked, biting her lip to stop it from quivering.

"Not at all," Leo amended hastily. "You know how much I care. It's just that I'm not a manager. I really don't know anything about lumber—or farming for that matter. Now horses...that's something I do know about."

"So...you still think I should sell."

The words stuck in Diane's throat. Her whisper was more a statement than a question.

"I think you ought to consider it at least," he answered gravely.

Seeing the sparkle of tears in her eyes, Leo took her in his arms again. "I know it's hard even to imagine doing it, darling, but you know how much I want you to be happy."

"I'm happy here at Black Oaks, Leo," Diane said fiercely, pulling away from him and brushing away the tear that was sliding down her cheek. "Grandmother must have thought I could handle it, or she never would have left it to me."

No sooner had she spoken the words than a vivid picture of Martin Leblanc sprang up before her. Suddenly she had an intense longing to see the nocturnal stranger again. *He understands*, she thought, *and he knows I can do it.*

Diane felt her lips trembling again and the tears once more gathering in her eyes. She turned away from Leo and walked over to stare out the window.

"I didn't mean to upset you, Diane," Leo said soothingly, putting an arm around her shoulders. "Don't give it another thought. I have to go now, but remember what I said about locking up the silver. Why don't you make yourself some tea, then go off to bed—you look exhausted. Goodnight, my sweet."

Leo dropped a kiss on the side of her neck, then left.

There was a time, not so long ago, when I shivered with pleasure whenever Leo kissed me, Diane thought to herself, still staring out the window. *Now—it's odd—I feel nothing. What's changed?*

Diane watched her fiancé until he disappeared into the shadows. Then she slowly walked back to the table.

She started to sit down again to her work but was drawn back to the window, where she stood gazing out at the night. Her thoughts were far from all the precau-

tions Leo wanted her to take in order to protect herself
and her silver.

She was thinking of something much more immediate and eminently more practical. Black Oaks' heavy,
old-fashioned silver was, indeed, very valuable. If she
sold some of it, she would have enough money to meet
this month's expenses. In fact, if Leo's estimate of its
worth was correct, she would only have to sell one or
two pieces to get the amount she needed.

That extra cash would tide her over until fall, when
she would receive not only the income from the harvest, but also payment for a big shipment of timber
that her grandmother had already arranged to sell.

Of course, she remembered, her grandmother had
verbally earmarked the profits from the latter transac-
tion for her granddaughter's wedding trousseau. The
older woman had been determined that Diane's trousseau be at least as beautiful as her own had been.

However, Diane decided, her own situation was very
different from that of her grandmother as a young
bride and that she would be betraying no trust if she
used that money to keep the estate going. She didn't
mind giving up part of her trousseau, in fact, she felt
she could do without a great many things usually found
in a bride's dowry. The old cupboards of Black Oaks
were already filled to overflowing with beautiful linen,
china and crystal, and that was all she really needed.
Besides, keeping the account books in the black was
much more important.

Leo wasn't marrying her for her belongings anyway,
she told herself. If he preferred the easy life to the struggle that must be waged to work the land, that was
because of the way he'd been brought up. He wasn't

interested in Black Oaks now, but if she held the estate together for a time, maybe after they were married, he would change and throw his energy into helping her make a success of the vast enterprise.

As she sat there at the long dining room table, her head in her hands, Diane tried to be honest with herself. Something inside her warned her not to indulge in silly daydreams.

Since her grandmother had died, Leo seemed to have changed radically. What had happened to the promise he'd made to throw himself body and soul into Black Oaks and help her run the estate as well as it had been in her grandmother's day? For him even to suggest she think of selling the place was a clear indication he didn't understand how she felt at all and he never would. For him, living at Wildacres was a passing phase in his life, something temporary. He undoubtedly found it pleasant, but he could probably be equally happy in any place that offered equal comforts. He had not really even grown up there. He had no ties to his home at Wildacres, no feeling for the place at all.

But Black Oaks, to Diane, was a different story. Black Oaks represented ten generations of Bernards. Thanks to its solid structure and the upkeep that had been scrupulously attended to over the years, the old house had withstood the ravages of time admirably. Over the centuries, the house had witnessed every kind of emotion, every kind of human experience. The last dying breath of an old master, the first cry of a newborn child, the laughter of happy times, the tears of struggle and, at times, defeat—the house had known them all. History and the emotions of the people who had carved it out were still in the walls and in the very air she breathed. Ten generations of Bernards had left their imprint on the house, and it was all the greater for that.

But Leo wasn't part of all that. He was like a bird sitting on a branch of a great tree. And she was in the branch of that tree, whose roots ran deep into the earth that had fed them. Leo would never understand this, she realized.

Suddenly she felt frightened. She did love Leo. . .but perhaps she loved him more like a brother than a fiancé. . . .

Maybe Leo was right after all. . .maybe that *was* the way she felt about him. At times, she did feel indulgent toward him, but she'd never been so madly in love with him that she'd been blinded to his faults. It had never been like that for her, and now, ultimately she was thankful she could see him so clearly.

Chapter 11

As Diane remained gazing out the window lost in thought, the sweet, delicately scented night air flooded into the room. The big, amber-colored moon rose in the sky, moving slowly behind the dark filagree of the leaves on the trees outside. The brown tile roof of the house must look beautiful in the pale yellow moonlight, she thought.

Suddenly the door swung open, casting a shaft of light across the room, and Germaine walked in. "What are you doing here in the dark, miss? You gave me the scare of my life. I've just finished closing up all the shutters for the night, and I'm on my way to bed. Are you going to bed soon?"

"Not just yet."

Germaine proceeded to close the shutters and, before leaving the room, turned and looked at Diane once more. "Are you all right, miss? Is there anything I can get you?"

"I'm fine, thanks, Germaine."

When Germaine had left, Diane stacked the account books and legal papers and carried them to the study. Then she returned to the dining room and opened the doors of the massive sideboard. She reached inside and took out several very ornate silver dishes and put the heavy pieces on the table.

She was holding a particularly lovely silver vegetable dish up to the light when suddenly she heard three short knocks at the window. The table was covered with antique silver, and the sideboard cupboard door was lying open, revealing all the treasures inside. For a moment she panicked.

Then, remembering the startlingly clear image in her mind just a little while earlier, she walked quickly over the front door and opened it for Martin Leblanc.

As he walked through the hall into the dining room, his eyes swept over the glittering silver spread out on the table. "It looks as if you were expecting me," he said, his eyes twinkling. "I've always had an eye for beautiful things."

He held out his hand to her and, ignoring her obvious dismay, walked straight over to the table. He picked up a tankard, examined it closely for a moment and then pointed to the Bernard coat of arms engraved on the side. "This is a real museum piece you've got here. Do you have more?"

"A few," she replied hesitantly.

Trying to appear relaxed and unconcerned, she walked slowly over to the sideboard and closed the cupboard door. When she turned and came back to the table, Martin was looking at her, a mocking light in his eyes.

"Aren't you afraid they'll gather dust in there?" he asked.

Diane flushed. "Maybe," she replied, a faint quiver in her voice. "But it's perhaps wiser than leaving them on display. Someone might be tempted to...."

"Believe me, Diane," Martin interrupted, "if a thief decided to make away with the family treasures, there wouldn't be all that much you could do about it. He could open any lock he wanted. Let me see that key for a minute, will you please?"

After hesitating for a second, she held it out to him.

For a moment, he examined it closely and then gave it back to her. "It's a very old lock and could easily be forced if necessary."

"You seem very knowledgeable about such things," she said coolly.

"A simple question of insatiable curiosity, my lovely," Martin replied, smiling. "Haven't you noticed that about me? But come on, tell me how things are going. Aren't you going to ask me to sit down, by the way?"

Diane felt vaguely uneasy and didn't quite know what to say. "I'm surprised to see you. I didn't think I would ever see you again."

"Not even when I promised you I would be back?"

Diane preceded her visitor into the living room. "I've had so much on my mind, I...please, sit down," she said haltingly, motioning him to the big armchair. The dogs, who had followed them, curled contentedly at his feet.

She sat down opposite him and took a deep breath. "I didn't realize you were still in the area."

"I've just come back, actually. But that's enough about me. Let's talk about you. How is the farm going?"

"Well, things aren't going very well," she replied in a discouraged voice. "But I love Black Oaks too much to give in and sell it."

"Are you trying to tell me you're having money troubles?" he asked, staring at her.

She bowed her head and said nothing.

"And you need to get your hands on some ready cash, right?" he asked. Then he motioned toward the dining room, where Diane could not forget the ornate, heavy silverware spread out on the table. "You're thinking of selling some of your silver, aren't you?"

"Yes," she said simply. "I have a lot of bills I have to pay by the end of the month."

"You are having a rough time of it, aren't you?" he said quietly. "That's a difficult decision you're faced with. Some of those pieces must have been in your family for centuries."

"Yes, they have. I don't quite know how I'm going to bring myself to sell any of them. I can hardly bear the thought of letting them go out of the family. Selling any one of those beautiful pieces almost feels like selling part of myself. And I've had no experience with dealers in this sort of thing, so I'm afraid I'll be cheated."

"May I give you a piece of advice, Diane?" Martin asked softly.

"Yes...please. I would appreciate any help I could get," she replied, suddenly feeling ashamed of her reaction when he first arrived.

"I have had experience with this sort of thing. The tankard I looked at when I came in is worth a great deal of money. If you gave it to me, I could get you a very good price for it. It would pay the men's wages for this month, I should think, and you would have a little breathing space."

"That's a wonderful idea. Take it, by all means," she exclaimed.

"You really are pressed for money, aren't you?" he said, more as a statement than a question.

"Yes, I am," she admitted. "I don't have any more cash on hand, and on the first of the month, I have to pay a tax installment as well as wages to the farm-hands, lumberjacks and servants."

Diane suddenly felt strangely relieved. At last she could talk to someone who cared, someone who was willing to share the problems that weighed so heavily on her slender shoulders. She felt Martin understood everything, even when she didn't explain all the details. She even found herself telling him things she had deliberately kept from Leo. Martin's reactions to her statements were so different...so supportive....

She told him about Gerardy's defiance, about the pilfering by so many of the men and about the ongoing problem with the poachers. Occasionally he interrupted with a question or a comment, but mostly he just listened. Diane felt that in Martin she'd found the friend she'd lost in her grandmother.

She finished speaking, and for a long time the two of them sat in the living room in a warm enveloping silence.

After a time, Martin spoke. "I think your analysis of the situaion is quite correct. You certainly have problems, but it's not a disaster. Your main trouble is cash flow—you have to have some money to keep the estate operating until it shows a profit. That's something everyone who works the land faces from time to time.

"Now," Martin continued, "there are a number of ways to get money quickly. I'm sure your lawyer has described several of them. But one of the fastest would be to sell some of those pretty things in the dining room. It's a shame to lose any of them, but it's better than giving up the land for want of a little ready cash.

"So," he continued, "I'll take the tankard and bring you the money. And meanwhile, you just keep right on doing what you've been doing. You are on the right track, and a man like Gerardy will probably trip himself up before he harms you." He smiled, then smothered a yawn.

"You're tired," exclaimed Diane. "I'll get you a blanket so you can sleep in the study."

When she returned from upstairs, she found Martin in the dining room, putting two tankards into his knapsack.

"I've taken two of them, Diane. I hadn't realized you had a tax bill to pay as well as the men's wages." He finished tying the knapsack. "You'd better put the rest back in the sideboard," he said with a mocking smile, pointing to the silver on the table.

Remembering the conversation she'd had with Leo that afternoon, Diane was suddenly overcome with fear and, giving into a feeling of imminent danger, she warned Martin not to go near Wildacres.

He turned around abruptly and stared down at her. He looked completely different, his face tense and white, his mouth drawn into a thin tight line. "How well do you know those people over there?" he asked, not at all surprised at her strange request.

"I'm engaged to Leo Marchand. Wildacres is his parents' home."

She didn't dare say that all the inhabitants of Wildacres were ready to shoot anyone who looked vaguely suspicious.

Martin was obviously startled at her announcement.

For a moment he just stared at Diane. Then he leaned toward her, took her hand in his and brought it to his lips. When he straightened, he had regained his composure but was perceptibly withdrawn. "Don't worry," he said finally, "I won't go near the place."

Had he planned to rob Wildacres as he had the Richards' place, she wondered frantically. She didn't know what to think anymore. She remained standing, caught in a web of conflicting feelings, and sighed wearily.

Martin kept staring at her as if he wanted to memorize every feature of her face, to etch into his mind the picture of her standing in front of him, small and slim, her lovely face reflecting an anguish he couldn't understand.

Slowly he walked over to the spot where she was standing in the doorway. His eyes still intent on her, holding her gaze, he slowly put his arms around her and pulled her to him. First he kissed her temple gently, next her eyelids, her cheeks.

Then his mouth came down on hers, and his arms tightened around her. He kissed her passionately, crushing her lips with an urgency that left Diane breathless. Finally, he released her. "I won't apologize for that," he said softly.

Trembling, Diane pulled away and without a word ran upstairs to the sanctuary of her bedroom.

Chapter 12

Hours later, Diane lay awake in bed. She could still feel Martin's lips on hers. His face swam before her eyes, and she remembered his every word, every gesture throughout the evening.

What is happening to me, she asked herself over and over again. *I'm engaged to Leo Marchand!* But she knew that Leo's lips had never burned their impression on her own the way Martin's had. Never had her body caught fire as it had when Martin embraced her.

Another thought kept Diane awake as well. The possibility—however remote—that Martin could be the thief whom Leo had been talking about tortured her with anxiety. She couldn't believe it. She kept seeing Martin's strong, sensitive face, his tender concern that appeared in his eyes whenever he looked at her, his sympathy that filled her with a sense of well-being both sweet and painful. Some kind of bond had sprung up between them, and when he was with her, she experienced a joy she'd never known with Leo. She could talk to Martin, confide in him. But with Leo, she always had to hold back, pretend, hide her feelings.

The silence in the room was stifling. Once there was a loud creaking sound that seemed to come from downstairs, but it only served to make the subsequent quiet more palpable. Diane remembered that, as a very small child, she had been terrified by the creaking of the wood paneling cooling off after a hot day. Now it was just one of the many familiar sounds in Black Oaks.

Finally, through the window, Diane saw dawn lightening the sky, its first pearl gray streaks, faintly tinged with pink to indicate the approaching sunrise.

And finally she saw the truth that she'd fought against all night. She wasn't in love with Leo at all. She doubted she ever had been. She was in love with Martin Leblanc.

And here she was, caught in a terrible dilemma. She'd known Leo for fifteen years, loved him—or so she thought. Now suddenly, all those years counted for nothing, they were gone. As she felt her feelings for Leo slip away and dissolve into nothing, she found herself being drawn more and more toward Martin, a complete stranger.

As she was getting dressed a little while later, Diane heard a commotion downstairs. She could hear doors opening and closing, and the echo of quick footsteps on the tiled floors.

Suddenly she heard Marthe's voice loud and clear over the others. "Good heavens, come quick, Miss Diane! We've been robbed! The sideboard with all the silver in it has been broken into! What are we going to do? I can't believe it!"

Diane swayed slightly as she stood on the landing.

Waves of shock ran through her body. She'd been tricked, fooled, used. She could hardly believe it. For a moment, she felt nauseous and thought she was going to faint. She reached back to the wall for support and leaned there for a minute trying to get hold of herself. Then, as if in a dream, she heard Germaine's voice from the floor below.

"Those beautiful silver tankards, Miss Diane, the ones Mrs. Bernard loved so much!" The woman wailed. "They're gone—all six of them.

Diane's legs almost buckled under her as she made her way downstairs, hardly feeling the floor beneath her feet.

"It was the shutter. It doesn't lock properly," Germaine said more calmly as Diane walked into the dining room. "I was thinking about that last night when I was closing it—thinking that Charles ought to have a look at it. There are two others like it. With the same damaged hasp. The thief must have tried different windows until he found this one."

As Diane entered the room, the two servants ran to her, interrupting each other as they described the loss.

"Oh, Miss Diane," wailed Germaine. "I feel just like Marthe. I won't sleep a wink until that man is caught."

Facing the two distraught servants, Diane forced herself to remain calm, pushing her own emotions firmly to the back of her mind, she surveyed the room with as much objectivity as she could muster.

"He took exactly what he wanted and nothing more," she told them evenly. "He had all the time in the world to choose what he would take, so he probably won't be back again."

"Oh, I doubt that, miss," Marthe cried. "He couldn't

carry everything with him at once. But he saw everything we have here, and he'll be back for more, mark my words. What nerve—he didn't even try to hide what he'd done. The door of the sideboard was lying wide open and everything inside was topsy-turvy when I came in this morning."

The old lock had been so easy to force, she thought ironically. How stupid she'd been! He was probably laughing at her right now. She'd been so naive, and trusting.

Diane felt sick as she remembered all the things she'd told Martin. She pictured the concerned look on his face—his apparent interest in her problems. *It was all just so much bait to allay my fears and suspicions*, she thought miserably.

"Charles doesn't know yet," Marthe announced. "But when he comes back from his rounds and finds out, he'll feel just as awful about this as we do. Those beautiful tankards—I remember Mrs. Bernard saying they were worth all the rest of the silver put together. We must call the police right away."

"Yes, we must do that immediately," Diane replied mechanically.

"Marthe, would you go out and find Charles and tell him I want to see him right away? Tell him also that I want to speak to Gerardy."

"What I can't understand," Germaine said suddenly, "is the dogs. They were sleeping right here in the dining room and didn't make a sound. Neither of the dogs is friendly toward strangers, so what on earth happened? None of us heard them barking during the night. It's strange . . . very strange."

"They say good burglars have some kind of power

over dogs," Marthe commented as she walked toward the door. "The Richards have dogs, too, but they didn't stop the burglar from getting in and taking everything he could get his hands on."

Diane remembered how silent the dogs had been during each of Martin's visits. She'd attributed their silence to their instinctive recognition of someone who was good and friendly. But it was obviously something else they'd sensed. . . .

"Won't Mister Leo be surprised when he finds out what happened," Germaine commented. "Just last night, he was telling us we didn't have anything to worry about over here. I remember he said that Black Oaks was so far off the beaten track, no thief would ever find us. Charles said he thought so, too. Little did they know!"

"When did Leo tell you that?" Diane asked in surprise.

"Last night." He came straight into the kitchen for a cool drink and told us all about the robbery over at the Richards. Then, after he'd given us the news, he realized we were all afraid and upset by it and tried to make us feel better by telling us we would be safe over here."

"He probably . . . . Oh, look, there's Charles now," Diane said, glancing out the window. But as the figure drew nearer she realized, to her surprise, that it was Gerardy.

The overseer walked straight through the kitchen into the dining room without knocking or putting out the cigarette that dangled from the corner of his mouth.

"Did you want to talk to me about reseeding the south fields?" he asked, a bored expression on his face. "I got them all done, day after I saved the hay."

"I know all I need to know about the south fields *and* the hay," she replied calmly. "What I would like you to explain, however, is why you had Beauval cut down those saplings without my permission."

"For the fences you ordered," he answered contemptuously. "Do you expect me to build them out of nothing?"

"There's plenty of old wood around the farm you could have used. You have no right to go into the forest and cut trees there, and you're well aware of that."

He stood there silently for a moment, rolling the cigarette butt around between his teeth. "Was it your robber friend who ratted on me?" he asked insolently, staring at her fixedly.

"My robber friend? What on earth do you mean?"

"I've got eyes in my head," he said, a leer on his face. "It was just about eleven o'clock last night wasn't it, miss? I don't miss nothing, you know. When a stranger goes into a lady's house late at night, well, that's something to take note of, isn't it? Especially when you hear the next day that there was a robbery in the very same house."

Diane felt the blood drain from her face as she stood rooted to the spot in front of him, her heart beating wildly in her chest. She couldn't take her eyes off his face. He was smirking down at her, his eyes glinting with a perverse kind of pleasure at her obvious discomfort.

"The man who came to see me last night had nothing to do with the burglary," Diane answered, trying to keep her voice from trembling. "But I don't owe you any explanations, Gerardy. What goes on in my house is none of your business."

"Well, maybe it isn't," he said, shifting from one foot to the other. "But I bet Mister Leo would have something to say about all this, if he found out."

"Well, if you're all that interested in his reaction, why don't you tell him," she replied coldly. "Listen, Gerardy, I don't intend, now or at any time in the future, to discuss my private affairs with you. Now, as for this business about the saplings, I would advise you to read the terms of your contract very carefully. It says very clearly that you are not allowed to cut down any trees in the forest without my express permission. If I ever find you doing such a thing again, I'll report you to the police for trespassing."

"That's fine with me," he said, shrugging indifferently. "But just remember, if the cows wander out of the pasture, and the ducks get into the garden because I don't have enough wood to build proper fences to keep them in, that's your tough luck. You gotta make up your mind what you want," he added, as he threw her a contemptuous glance. Then he turned and strode out of the room.

Diane was still shaking from her encounter with the overseer when there was a discreet knock on the door.

"Come in," she said.

It was Charles. He walked in slowly, holding his cap in his hand, his kindly face drawn and tense.

"I just saw Gerardy leave, miss. Was he being just as difficult and uncooperative as usual?"

"I'm afraid so, Charles. I told him about the saplings, and he offered a very lame excuse and strode out of here, arrogant as you please." Diane sat down wearily. "Marthe told you about the burglary, I suppose?"

"Yes, she told me that some of the silver had been

taken—the tankards I think she said—and that you wanted me to call the police. I can't understand it, miss. I'm a very light sleeper. I'm sure I would have heard someone trying to get in, and yet . . . ."

"Dear Charles," she said warmly, "please don't worry about it. There's nothing any of us could have done. It was probably my fault anyway."

As she had started speaking, Diane had decided it would be better to come right out and tell Charles about her visits from Martin rather than let the kindly old man get a distorted picture from all the idle gossip that Gerardy would certainly initiate around the farm.

She asked the gamekeeper to sit down for a moment and quietly proceeded to tell him about the two visits from her mysterious night traveler. Charles listened carefully as she told her story and didn't interrupt her once.

"He's probably the man I saw this morning," he said when she had finished.

"You saw him? Where? How?" she exclaimed, staring in amazement at the old man, her dark eyes glowing intensely.

"I went out this morning around dawn," he began. "I know Gerardy has laid some rabbit traps at the edge of the woods, and I was hoping to catch him in the act of checking them."

In his slow, ponderous manner, Charles described walking toward the woods and coming upon a man taking pictures. Charles had assumed the stranger was a friend of Diane's because he had asked about her and had appeared to know about her engagement to Leo.

"Maybe it was the thief," Charles remarked, after he'd finished recounting the incident. "Who knows? I

did notice his pockets were bulging a bit. And then
again, maybe he wasn't the one at all. He had such an
honest face, I couldn't picture him stealing anything. If
you don't want me to, Miss Diane, I won't tell the
police about him."

"What on earth was he taking pictures for?" Diane
asked in unabashed curiosity, the theft temporarily
pushed right out of her mind.

"He said he was a bird-watcher, miss," Charles
replied. "He told me that he loves going out in the early
morning and walking in the woods. And he said he was
something of an amateur photographer as well.

"About the police, miss," Charles continued as Diane
remained silent. "Shall I phone for them?"

Diane hesitated for a moment. If she called the
police, there would be all kinds of very unfavorable
publicity, which would only reflect back on her. And
yet, Gerardy already knew about the theft and would
talk for sure—there was no way she could stop him.

"Yes, I think that would be best, Charles," she said
quietly. "We really don't have the right to keep it to
ourselves, do we? Besides, Gerardy saw Mr. Leblanc
last night when he was coming into the house, so. . . ."

The old man threw a quick glance in her direction.
"Gerardy saw him!" he exclaimed. "Well, I'm not surprised. That troublemaker was probably out checking
his rabbit snares. But that's a bit of bad luck, his seeing
all that, isn't it, miss? He's a bad lot that one, and he'd
use something like that against you at the drop of a hat.
And you never know what he'll add to the story to
make it more interesting."

Charles fell silent for a moment, his brow lined with
concentration. "Miss Diane," he said finally. "What if

we say that the man who came to see you last night was a nephew of mine who was visiting Black Oaks? Marthe and Germaine would go along with the story—I know they would."

"No, I don't think that's such a good idea, Charles," she said, after a slight pause, "but thank you anyway. I don't think we should start telling lies about all this. I did something stupid, and I'm just going to have to take the consequences."

"And what about Mister Leo?" he asked shyly.

"I'll have to tell him the truth too," she replied miserably.

Chapter 13

"What's all this talk about some man visiting you late at night?" Leo shouted a short while later as he stormed into the living room where Diane was sitting quietly looking out the window.

"What's going on around here?" he continued at the top of his voice. "What are you thinking of, letting strange men walk into your house in the dead of night? And what kind of a man would come here . . . take your hospitality . . . then rob you blind? This is incredible! You let a man you don't even know in the house and the next morning all your silverware is gone!"

Leo was silent for a minute as he paced the length of the room, then he resumed shouting. "Why, in God's name, didn't you tell me about this fellow? After all, I am the man you're going to marry. I can't understand why you kept something like this from me . . . unless, of course . . . unless you had something to hide."

Diane, who was sitting in a chair by one of the windows that faced the front of the house, turned and slowly got to her feet. "If you don't trust me, Leo, then I think we should break our engagement," she added in a clear, firm voice.

"If I don't trust you," he cried. "I don't know if I trust you or not. What in God's name is going on here anyway? I feel as if I'm going crazy. I put complete trust and confidence in you, Diane, and now I learn from a man I hardly know that you've been entertaining a strange man behind my back in the middle of the night. You should have told me about this yourself—at least made some attempt at explaining what happened."

"Oh, so Gerardy ran to you with the story, did he?"

"Yes, he did," he said furiously. "Please note, however, that I didn't ask him to come. He came of his own free will, to tell me what he'd seen with his own eyes. He said I had a . . . a right to know what my fiancée was up to. You realize, of course, how distasteful and embarrassing the whole interview was for me, Diane."

"Yes, I understand perfectly. Just as I understand Gerardy's reason for running to you with his dirty little story."

"Well, do you deny it?"

"Why deny the truth? I don't make a habit of lying, you know that, Leo."

"But, in heaven's name, what possessed you to allow that kind of a man into your house? The lowest of the low—a common thief. How could you do such a thing?"

"I'm not so sure he was 'the lowest of the low,' as you put it," she retorted. "However, I had my reasons," she added, sitting down again in her chair by the window.

"Would you please explain to me exactly why he

came here?" Leo asked sounding out each word as if he were speaking to a child.

"He wanted shelter from the storm."

"Shelter from the storm," he exclaimed in stunned amazement. "But the only storm we've had was over a week ago!"

Leo paused, as if to assimilate what he had heard. With an effort to control his voice, he continued. "All right, tell me the truth. How many times did he come back after that?" he asked, his cold, blue eyes fixed intently on her pale face.

"Only once. That was last night," she replied wearily.

"And this time you welcomed him into your house with open arms for no reason at all. . . . Why didn't you say anything to me? You've got to explain what this is all about."

"There's nothing very mysterious about him," Diane replied softly.

Briefly she told Leo who the visitor had been, repeating what Martin had told her—that he was touring the region—and she explained that they had become friends during their two encounters.

"I don't feel badly about what I've done but I knew that if I told you, you would get furious. Obviously," she concluded, "I wasn't mistaken."

"Goodness knows, I've got good reason to be angry. Your cavalier attitude is astounding. I would never have believed you could be like this. You have all the proof anyone could need that this man is the burglar everyone is looking for; he proved it to you beyond any doubt and still you refuse to believe he's the one."

Diane made no reply. Leo paced up and down the

room, shaking his head. Then he stopped in front of Diane.

"He must have really hoodwinked you if you can't see him for the scheming crook he really is," Leo continued finally. "He undoubtedly had it all worked out. He probably cased out the land and the house long before he came here that night—made friends with the dogs, got to know the habits of people who lived in the house and on the farm so he could time his visit without being caught. Then, the first time he came, he could be sure of having just you to work on when he pretended to be seeking shelter from the storm. That way he was free to use every trick in the book to inspire you with confidence. Isn't that the way it happened? Well, isn't it, Diane?"

Diane silently bowed her head. She was in agony. Everything Leo was saying made complete sense, but she still couldn't believe it was true.

"There, you see?" he cried triumphantly. "You know that's the way it was. It's written all over your face. Then, a week later, he comes back, and this time he takes everything he'd come for in the first place. You just won't face it, will you? You refuse to see what's staring you right in the face. I don't know what's the matter with you, Diane, unless . . . ."

"Unless what?"

Leo sat down opposite her and buried his face in his hands. "I'd like to strangle that man. Right now, I can't think of anything that would give me greater pleasure."

"Jealousy is such a primitive, useless emotion, especially when there's no reason for it," she said wearily.

Leo lifted his head and looked over at her. She looked pale, worn out, at the end of her rope. "What's going on between you and that man?" he said brutally. "You look completely exhausted, and I want to know why. If there's a reason for you to look so unhappy, I want to know it—I have a right to know."

"There's nothing between us," Diane replied, her voice nearly a whisper.

Leo walked toward her and looked down at her, his blue eyes as cold as ice. "Do you realize just how deeply you have compromised yourself by this ridiculous escapade? Can you see what an untenable position you've put both of us in? Well, I'm going to get us out of it somehow. I promised your grandmother I would look after you, and that's exactly what I'm going to do."

An uncomfortable silence grew between them. Finally Leo broke it, speaking with controlled fury.

"You can't stay alone here any longer, you realize," he said. "You're coming to Wildacres with me. I can't take you today because I've got to go to Paris. But as soon as I get back, you're coming home with me, and we'll get married from there as soon as possible. From now on, I'll take care of everything. We've got to stop the rumors once and for all. We won't report the theft to the police—"

"We have to, Leo," Diane said quietly, infinite weariness in her voice. "Charles has already phoned them. They'll be here any minute."

"There was no need to call them, Diane," Leo said harshly. "We could have handled this ourselves. Well, we'll just have to tell them we found the tankards and that it was all a mistake. We certainly don't want everyone in the area to hear of your crazy nocturnal escapades."

"Oh, I think we're too late to put a stop to that particular news item," she laughed mirthlessly. "I imagine Gerardy has posted bulletins by now."

"I find your humor not only unamusing, Diane, but in very poor taste," Leo said coldly. "The only thing to do is to get married right away and minimize the damage as best we can."

"I...I can't marry you, Leo," Diane said slowly. "It would never work."

Leo whirled around and stared at her. "Nonsense, Diane," he said sharply. "You're just upset. I...admit I may have overreacted a little to this incident, but nothing has changed my feelings for you."

"I said it won't work Leo. You'll never feel the way I do about Black Oaks."

"Be reasonable, darling," Leo said, his voice softening. "I realize it'll be a wrench at first, but you'll get over it. Eventually you'll be glad you sold."

Diane sat, his voice battering her. Apparently Leo took her failure to protest as his cue to continue.

"I've thought about it a great deal," he said firmly. "I think we should sell the house, its grounds and part of the farm for starters. We can divide the rest into lots—we'll get a lot more money doing it that way. I already have a buyer for the house and the farm, someone who is prepared to pay cash.

"Diane," Leo said, his assertiveness seeming to flag after the forceful monologue he had just delivered. "I've...asked this fellow—the prospective buyer, I mean—to come by tomorrow and have a look at the place."

At the look of consternation on Diane's face, he added quickly, "Just let him look around, and then find out how much he's willing to pay, sweetheart, that's all you have to do. There's no need to make a decision right away. Ah...he'll be around sometime in the afternoon, okay?

"Now remember," Leo said after a momentary pause, "you don't have to commit yourself right away.

"But one of the things you should be thinking about is choosing the best three hundred acres of the estate to be divided up into lots fairly soon."

Diane was still unable to speak, but she shook her head slowly.

Leo was unrelenting. "You do realize, don't you, that if you follow my advice, you won't have any financial worries for the rest of your life? Listen, Diane. One way or the other, you're bound to end up selling. Putting it off any longer will only be more painful for you—believe me. You must be brave and act with courage now, my dear—for yourself, for me and for everyone who is depending on you. Just think about it, that's all I ask."

AFTER LEO HAD GONE, the police arrived to get full details of the theft. Then a multitude of routine business details had to be dealt with, all with the thought that Leo might be carrying her off to Wildacres in two days' time. It was early evening before Diane was finally alone.

Just think about it. Leo's words kept echoing in her ears. To whom could she turn for advice, Diane asked herself miserably, as she crawled into bed a little while later, exhausted from the day's events. She'd called the lawyer Mr. Garnier earlier in the week and discussed the financial situation of Black Oaks with him. They'd talked about the possibility of mortgaging the estate to raise some capital, but during the last few days Diane had been too busy to set up an appointment with the bank.

Maybe Leo is right after all, Diane thought wretchedly. *Maybe Black Oaks is too much for me to handle.*

Well, I'll talk to the prospective buyer Leo said was coming by tomorrow, she resolved. *I feel incapable of making a decision now.* Her thoughts became vague, and Diane drifted into a deep, dreamless sleep.

Chapter 14

"I'm off on my rounds, now, Miss Diane," Charles said to her the next morning, just as she was beginning her breakfast.

"If you wait two minutes, I'll join you," Diane replied, hurriedly drinking her coffee.

"A pleasure indeed, miss. It's been a long time since we've walked through the estate together."

Diane downed the last of her coffee quickly. As she and Charles went out the back door, her Irish setters came bounding up, pleading to be taken for a run.

Reluctantly Diane ordered them away. She loved their company, but she knew she'd be walking mostly in the forest, where the dogs could not help but frighten the animals.

The setters banished, Diane and Charles walked through the garden toward the forest to begin their tour of the estate. Once in the woods, they walked companionably through the trees, discussing the lumber situation in general, but referring frequently to the poachers. The problem had improved temporarily after the wardens had caught two of them the night of her grandmother's death. But within two weeks they'd returned in full force, shamelessly trapping as many animals as they could.

"They're brazen, those poachers, miss. It seems that not even the game wardens can scare 'em away."

"I know, Charles," Diane sighed, "but we have to keep trying." After a while they left the main path and began to weave through the trees on less-used paths that meandered about, making the forest into one huge labyrinth.

As they rounded one enormous oak, its trunk easily five feet in diameter, Charles suddenly gasped. He stopped dead in his tracks, and Diane, mystified by the old man's reaction, walked past him to find out what he was staring at.

She stopped, too, staring in horror at the body of deer ensnared in a sharp-toothed metal trap. The flesh around the animal's neck had been almost shredded by its last, frantic efforts to get free.

To Diane, that carcass seemed to represent the futility of her managerial efforts at Black Oaks. She leaned against the tree trunk behind her and closed her eyes. Even if the bank did lend her a sizable amount of money, she thought, she doubted she'd ever be able to manage the estate properly.

I'll think about it later, she said to herself firmly. *Now there's work to be done.*

"Let's remove the carcass, Charles," Diane said calmly to the gamekeeper. "There's no need for the poachers to benefit more than necessary."

With a great effort, Charles reached up and pulled

the trap down from the branch to which it was attached. The weight of the carcass made the task very awkward. It took him a long time to remove the iron collar from the animal's neck; the trap was old and the springs had rusted.

At length he was able to free the animal's body, and the hinges sprang the empty trap shut, with a resounding snap. Heaving the carcass onto his back, Charles turned to Diane. "There's a pit about a hundred yards from here, miss," he said, his breath coming in short gasps. "I think I'd better take the deer over there and bury it as best I can."

"Thank you, Charles," Diane said quietly. "I'll wait for you here."

When the old man had shuffled off, Diane wandered along a little-used path that she knew ran back toward the edge of the forest. A dirt road ran between the peripheries of the forest and the farm at that point, and Diane stood idly watching a wagon full of hay creaking its way back from one of the fields. The farmer waved as he passed by.

A minute later, she saw a car approaching in the distance, billowing clouds of dust around it. As it came nearer, Diane saw with a start that it was Leo's car. Instinctively she edged back behind one of the massive tree trunks near where she stood.

Not fifty feet from where she was hidden the car stopped, and to her astonishment, Gerardy got out of the passenger side. With a nod to the driver, he began to walk down the road toward the farm. The car turned around and sped away, throwing up a spray of pebbles and dust in its wake.

What business do those two have together, Diane wondered, perplexed.

The thought was still troubling her when Charles returned and they resumed their walk together.

"Charles," she asked after they'd been walking a little while, "does Mister Leo have much contact with Gerardy? I mean, is Leo often at the farm?"

"Hard to say, miss, about business, you might say. But I have seen him and Gerardy talking together a few times. Why, miss?"

"Only that he's never mentioned having any real contact with Gerardy to me. In fact, it's been years since I've known Leo to be at Black Oaks except when he's visiting me."

Chapter 15

Black Oaks had never looked so beautiful, Diane thought that afternoon. The forest was at its verdant best, proudly displaying the seemingly infinite variety of its magnificent trees. In the bright, luminescent sunshine, the surrounding countryside was ablaze with brilliant greenery, and amidst all this beauty, the house stood quiet and peaceful in the full glory of summer.

Reluctantly Diane turned her attention back to the ledger spread out before her. She sat, cross-legged on her bed, surrounded by a sea of papers. Her forehead was wrinkled in concentration when she heard a knock on her bedroom door.

"Come in," she called absently.

"There's a man at the door, miss," Germaine said, her eyes wide with curiosity. "He said he wants to see you."

Diane suddenly remembered that Leo had told her the prospective buyer for Black Oaks was coming to talk to her today. The events of the morning had made her forget all about it.

"I think I know who it is, Germaine," Diane said resignedly, climbing off her bed and running a comb through her hair. "Tell him I'll be right down."

Straightening her shoulders and trying to assume an air of nonchalance she didn't feel, Diane went downstairs into the living room to meet her unwelcome visitor.

But when she reached the door she stopped dead, one hand flying to her mouth.

"Surprised to see me?" Martin asked, walking over to Diane. She remained frozen to the spot. "I told you I'd sell the tankards for you, remember?"

His voice was warm and soft, and slowly Diane moved to the sofa and sat down, never taking her eyes off the man before her. A minute before she had been absolutely numb; now she was acutely conscious of the loud pounding of her heart.

"I...I don't know what to say," she whispered haltingly. "I thought you were the buyer for Black Oaks...I didn't think...."

"The buyer for Black Oaks," Martin echoed in amazement. "Surely, Diane, you're not going to sell! After all you've been through.... What's happened while I was gone to make you suddenly decide to sell the one thing that means more to you than anything else in the world?"

As he was speaking he walked over to the sofa and sat down beside her, taking her hands in his.

Diane didn't answer his question immediately; her mind was awhirl with another thought. He couldn't possibly be the thief, she told herself. Her mind cried out that it wasn't true. She met his gaze, and as she looked at his strong, kind face and the understanding in his eyes, she was more convinced than ever that this man was no thief.

"Talk to me, Diane," Martin prodded gently. "What's happened?"

"It gets worse every day," she said in a small voice. "The poachers are ruining the forest; the men's pilfering is cutting into the profits; Gerardy is more insolent than ever; the first of the month is in three days, and I have no money to meet my taxes or the payroll."

"The tankards?" Martin murmured. "A stopgap measure, I know, but...."

"That's all it is—stopgap," Diane said miserably. "What good will it do in the long run to sell a couple of tankards to make ends meet? It's just putting off the inevitable," she said, conscious she was echoing Leo. "Before you know it, I'll have to sell something else and then something else, until everything I love has disappeared before my very eyes. I don't want to lose Black Oaks in bits and pieces like that—I couldn't stand it."

"But why are you looking on the dark side of everything?" Martin added, mild censure in his voice. "You're not like this. You're brave, courageous, strong—that's what I have admired about you right from the start. But maybe I was wrong...maybe you don't love the place the way you say you do."

With an anguished cry, Diane buried her face in her hands.

"I just can't see you living anywhere else," Martin continued. "And the reasons you're giving for leaving don't make any sense at all. They don't even sound like you. There's another reason why you're doing this, and you're not telling me what it is. I might be able to help you, Diane, but I can't do a thing for you if you won't tell me what's going on. I know you're having trouble with that overseer of yours—he's an evil man. But I also know you can find some way of getting rid of him if you want to, and he certainly won't be here forever. You're going through a bad time, but it will pass. I know how much you love this house, Diane."

Diane felt as if she was being torn in shreds. Leo's arguments had sounded reasonable the night before, but now Martin was saying what she'd been telling herself all along.

"You know, I grew up in a house that I loved, too," Martin said, getting up and walking over to the window. "It was a lot smaller and was by no means surrounded by a vast estate. But I loved it, and though we've been gone from it for fifteen years, the memory of it is still clear in my mind.

"Don't do what my parents were forced to do, Diane," Martin said, an edge to his voice. "Don't sell— you'll always regret it if you do."

"That's what I'm afraid of," Diane said softly, rising from the sofa and walking over to Martin's side. He put his arm around her and silently the two of them looked out the window down the long, tree-lined drive in front of the house.

The sound of the doorbell broke the silence in the room, and Diane could hear Germaine scurrying through the hall to answer the door.

She couldn't hear what the visitor said, but Germaine's shocked reply was quite audible. "You're what?" the maid gasped, and Diane turned to look at the doorway as Germaine hurried in.

"Miss Diane! There's a gentleman at the door who says he's going to buy Black Oaks! Shall I ask him to go away, miss?"

"Tell him it's sold," Martin said quickly, turning to face the old woman.

"Leo is going to be furious," Diane sighed after Germaine had left, a horrified expression on her face.

"Oh, so it was he who wanted you to sell," Martin commented, his voice growing hard.

"Yes, it was," she murmured. "Oh, he'd talked to me about selling once before, but then he didn't really insist when he saw how much it upset me to even think about it."

"And he thought you would feel differently about it now?" Martin asked ironically.

"Oh, well, enough of that for the moment," he continued, getting to his feet.

"You're obviously still not convinced I actually sold the tankards for you. Well, actions speak louder than words," he added, as he pulled a thick roll of bank notes out of his wallet. "Here's the money I got for them. I hope this will change your mind and give you the incentive to carry on."

"All that for two tankards?" she exclaimed.

"I told you they were worth a great deal of money. As you can see, I'm rarely mistaken about these things," he replied, a mocking light in his eyes.

"Listen, love, I have to go, but just tell me whether you're going to take my advice and fight for this place."

"Oh, please, don't go yet," cried Diane. "There's something I have to tell you. . . ."

Very slowly Diane took a step toward Martin, touched his arm and lifted her eyes to his. "Gerardy saw you come in the window the last time you were here," she said softly. "He told my fiancé."

"Who immediately flew into a jealous rage, right? And because of that, you let him convince you to sell?" Martin asked, his eyebrows arched in amazement.

"There was something else," Diane murmured, her eyes downcast.

Gently he pulled her close to him. "Go on," he said softly.

As she relaxed in his arms, she could smell a fresh, woodsy fragrance clinging to his jacket. Suddenly Diane was aware that he was kissing her hair. "Oh, Martin," she groaned, "I haven't any right to. . . ."

"Trust me, Diane," he whispered, his lips in her hair. "My conscience wouldn't allow me to take advantage of you or upset you in any way. Now, tell me what's on your mind."

She took a deep breath and began. "The morning you left, we discovered that the sideboard with all the silver in it had been broken into."

Martin withdrew from her slightly and looked down into her eyes. "Did you think I did it?"

"I didn't want to, but. . . ."

"And Gerardy didn't waste any time telling your fiancé that you'd been harboring criminals. . . . I'm beginning to understand now. Well, in a way, I guess I'm partly responsible for what happened."

He pushed her gently from him and took a couple of steps across the room, caught up in his thoughts. "Did the thief take everything?" he asked. "Did he leave you anything you can sell to get enough money to tide you over?"

"No, he didn't take everything. But he did take the rest of the tankards, the ones grandmother—"

"Were they like the two you gave me?" Martin broke in. "Were they engraved with the family coat of arms?"

"Yes," she replied. "Grandmother loved them most of all. That's why I gave you only two to sell. I couldn't bear parting with all of them."

Martin walked over to the window and looked out for a minute or two without speaking. When he turned and walked back to her, his face was hard, his expression resolute.

"I'm going to Paris," he announced. "But don't worry, I'll be back. I'm not going to leave you alone with all this. If you see your fiancé before I return, tell him you're not going to sell Black Oaks. Be very firm about it."

Diane nodded slowly. Martin gazed at her seriously, then spoke as though there was no change of topic.

"Where is your fiancé now, Diane?"

"He's in Paris," she replied, "but he should be back tomorrow."

"Whatever you do," said Martin solemnly, "don't give in to him again. Now listen, Diane, before I leave, I've got to ask you a rather personal question. It's absolutely essential you answer it as honestly as you can."

He leaned toward her and looked deep into her eyes. "Do you love Leo Marchand enough to marry him and spend the rest of your life as his wife?"

Diane felt the blood rush to her face. Somehow she knew that Martin's question represented a turning point in her life and that it was crucial that her answer be honest. She chose her words carefully.

"No, I don't think I have ever loved him that way," she replied slowly. "And, ever since he practically forced me to agree to sell Black Oaks, I haven't felt anything for him at all. But he was the only person I had left after my grandmother died, so I tried to make myself love him...but I can't. I...."

An undefinable expression flashed across Martin's face as he took her hands in his and pressed them to his lips. "He's not the only one in your life now," he said softly. "And one of these days, you're going to have to choose. But in the meantime, don't give in. Wait till I get back—I won't be gone long, I promise. Goodbye, Diane."

Chapter 16

After Martin had left, Diane went straight to the kitchen. She knew Marthe would be there preparing dinner and, like as not, Germaine would be sitting at the big table gossiping with her.

Diane smiled to herself as she imagined the buzz of animated chatter following Germaine's announcement to Marthe and Charles that someone had come to see Diane about buying Black Oaks. *They must be horrified*, she thought, *and terribly uncertain about the future. I'm going to have to put their minds at rest.*

Without preamble, Diane simply explained to Marthe and Germaine and to Charles—who had just come in—that, yes, after Leo had set forth his arguments so persuasively the night before, she had agreed to talk to a prospective buyer. At no point, however, had she made up her mind absolutely to sell.

"You three would have been among the first people to know if I had decided to sell," Diane declared vehemently. "I would never make such a grave decision without informing you immediately."

"Excuse me, Miss Diane," Germaine said, her forehead still creased with concern. "That first gentleman. He told me to tell the second gentleman that Black Oaks was already sold. Didn't he buy it then, after all?"

"He never intended to, Germaine. He simply wanted you to get rid of the customer that Mister Leo had sent over."

"Miss Diane," Charles said diffidently, "From Germaine's description of the first gentleman, he sounds like the chap I saw with the camera in the forest yesterday."

"That's right, Charles," Diane concurred. "They're one and the same."

"Do you think you should tell the police he's back, miss... I mean, just in case?"

"No, Charles," Diane said after a slight hesitation. "I don't think that will be necessary. Now, Marthe, let's all have a glass of wine from that carafe you've got on the table and toast the future of Black Oaks!"

DIANE AWOKE THE NEXT MORNING to a gray, overcast sky and the threat of an imminent storm. She scrambled into her clothes so she could do a bit of gardening before it started to rain, then hurried downstairs, telling Marthe she'd just have coffee and no breakfast.

She was glancing through the morning paper when the front doorbell rang. "I'll get it," she called to Germaine.

One of the policemen who had investigated the theft two days earlier tipped his hat to her. "Morning, Miss Bernard. We're still working on those burglaries. I wonder if I might look around again, just for a moment?"

"Of course," Diane said, standing aside to let him in.

"I won't be long, ma'am. I just want to check the windows and doors again."

Diane led the way into the dining room and returned to the table, where a steaming cup of coffee awaited her. She downed it quickly, her eyes watering with the heat, and was just about to go into the garden when the policeman called to her.

"Excuse me, ma'am, could you come over here for a minute please," he asked, standing in front of the door that led from the veranda off the dining room to the outside.

"We didn't notice this the first time," he said, looking embarrassed, "but there seems to be evidence here that this lock was tampered with."

Curious, Diane walked over to the screen door. When she peered closely at the wood around the bolt, she could see very slight scratches in the paint. "I never would have noticed," Diane said, looking up at the policeman. "Is this the work of a professional, do you think?"

"Well, not really, ma'am," the policeman replied. "Most of them usually cut the screen. It's faster—and quieter."

"This door, of course, would only get the thief into the veranda," Diane said practically. "He still had to open the door from here to the dining room."

"I've checked that door, as well, Miss Bernard. The lock on it has been forced, too."

"Why didn't you see this the first time you were here," Diane inquired mildly.

"Well, ma'am, by your maid's admission the window was unlocked when she went to open it that morning, and since the thief had entered by the windows in the other place, why we naturally thought. . . ."

"I see," Diane said impatiently. "Will that be all, officer?"

"Yes, ma'am," he mumbled. "Goodbye, ma'am."

With a relief that was overwhelming, Diane sat down on one of the dining-room chairs. This new evidence certainly exonerated Martin beyond question, she thought, with a sudden rush of pleasure; he had already been in the house that night and would have had no need to force any lock.

I knew he couldn't be the one, she said to herself. *I'll pay more attention to my instinct in future!*

In a cheery voice she called out to Marthe. "Any chance of another cup of your delicious coffee?" As Diane looked out the window, the rain started to teem down.

It stopped a little before lunchtime, and grabbing her trowel and basket, Diane walked through the sodden ground to work on the geraniums. She'd been in the garden for about an hour when Germaine came out to say that Mister Leo was in the living room, and as lunch was nearly ready, should she set a place for him at the table?

"Thank you, Marthe, if you're sure there's enough."

Wiping her hands on her jeans, Diane put away her gardening tools and went into meet her fiancé.

"Hello, darling," Leo greeted her, kissing her on the cheek. "Miss me?"

"Hello, Leo. How was Paris?"

"Great. I got everything accomplished I had to. I'm

pleased to be back though. I hate leaving the horses for any length of time. How's everything here?"

Deciding she might as well get the odious task over with, Diane took a deep breath and plunged in.

"Your prospective buyer came by yesterday," she said, keeping her voice casual.

"Oh, yes? How did it go?"

"I didn't sell. In fact, I've changed my mind about selling."

"What do you mean, Diane? I thought we'd been all through that."

"I've just given it some more thought, Leo, that's all. I'm keeping Black Oaks—I must have been mad to have even considered selling it."

"But do you know what you're saying?" he cried. "Surely you haven't forgotten what I told you? By letting that thief into your house, you've compromised yourself very badly. So we've got to get married quickly, and I've already told you it's impossible for me to live at Black Oaks even after we're married."

He paused only to catch his breath, then continued. "Besides, you haven't the money to keep the place going. It's madness to try and make it work. You're not thinking clearly, Diane. It's financial suicide for you to try to make a go of it," he shouted, making no attempt to hide his anger.

Diane said nothing but noted, with relief, that he seemed to have forgotten his threat to bear her off to his parents' house immediately. His mind was still on the sale she had refused.

"I'd found such a good deal for you too. It was a real bargain—you won't get another chance like it in a thousand years."

"I don't want another chance. I don't want to sell now or ever and that's final," she said quietly. "Something else you should know, Leo, is that the police were here again this morning."

Leo started, but Diane continued, ignoring his surprise. "There is conclusive evidence that Martin Leblanc couldn't possibly have stolen the tankards. He was already in the house when the theft occurred, and the policeman this morning discovered that the thief entered through the veranda off the dining room."

"Oh," Leo said coldly, "and just what did he find that was so convincing?"

"The locks on both doors had been jimmied," Diane replied coolly, "and the markings are new."

"Well, the damage has been done," Leo stated harshly. "This new evidence is a bit late to stop the gossip, don't you think?"

Just then Marthe announced that lunch was ready. In silence, Leo and Diane walked into the dining room. The atmosphere was strained, but Diane knew that there was no chance of her again relenting to Leo's arguments.

"We seem to have reached an impasse, Diane," Leo said, finally breaking the silence. "It looks as though I'm going to have to force the issue—you leave me no alternative.

"If you decide to keep Black Oaks—" Leo paused dramatically "—then I'm going to leave you to it. You'll just have to manage on your own, struggle to pay your bills on your own and face all the responsibilities and the shame you've brought on yourself on your own. So, choose—right here and now—and let's be done with it."

"There's no reason for me to be ashamed of anything I've done," she replied calmly. "My home is more important than anything or anyone." She turned to look him square in the face. "My choice has already been made, Leo. It's Black Oaks."

Leo stared back at her in stunned silence. Then, slowly replacing his fork on his plate he said, "You actually mean to say you'd take this...this financial suicide over me?"

"I think the lady means she is opting for the home she loves over a thief like yourself," a voice cut in. Diane whirled around to find herself face to face with Martin Leblanc, two silver tankards in his hand.

Chapter 17

"And who might you be?" Leo asked arrogantly, though visibly taken aback by Martin's entry. "And how dare you insinuate that . . ."

"I'm not insinuating anything," Martin returned calmly, ignoring Leo's first question. "What I am doing is accusing you of theft. The night in question, it was you who broke into this house—I'm not sure yet how—broke into the sideboard and took these two tankards. You then went to Paris and sold them to Mr. Marancourt, an antique dealer on Bac street. Can you prove I'm wrong?"

"Of course I can," Leo replied coldly. "That story's absurd . . . barely worthy of a reply. Why would I steal from my own fiancée? After our wedding, all this will be mine anyway. You'll never prove your crazy theory."

Diane noticed that as he spoke he never once looked at Martin, but kept his eyes fixed on the heavy, engraved tankards that had been placed on the table.

Martin turned toward Diane, his eyes demanding the truth.

"Do you believe him?" he asked simply.

"No, I don't, Martin," she replied firmly. "I don't believe one word of it."

"So this is your famous night visitor," Leo said scathingly, turning to Diane. "And you accuse me, too.. you would take the word of this total stranger over mine?"

"I won't be a stranger for long if that's what's worrying you," Martin interjected calmly.

"Thank you," he continued, turning to look at Diane. "Thank you for your confidence in me. I'm touched and very deeply grateful to you for that. So, you want proof, do you?" he said, turning back to Leo. "Well, I can't say I blame you. In your place, I would probably feel the same way."

Then, looking at Marthe and Germaine who had been standing by the door the whole time, their eyes wide with fear, he said, "Would one of you be kind enough to ask Mr. Marancourt to come in, please? He's waiting outside in the car."

Diane turned and looked at Leo. He was as white as a ghost and had bitten down so hard on his lower lip that it was bleeding. His eyes were riveted on the empty doorway. When he saw Mr. Marancourt come in, his whole manner betrayed him at once. He leaped to his feet, knocking over his wineglass, any vestige of composure completely gone.

"Mr. Marancourt," Martin began. "Do you see the man who sold you the tankards in this room?"

Wordlessly, the antique dealer pointed to Leo. "That's the gentleman over there, sir," Mr. Marancourt replied without the slightest hesitation. "We had a very long discussion about the money he wanted for the tankards. I recognized them as very old and valuable pieces right away, of course, but, even so, I ended up paying what I considered an exorbitant price for them. However, according to this gentleman, I was still not paying him what they were worth. But despite his opinion, I believe he got a very good deal."

"You must be mistaken," Leo said quickly, his voice trembling. "You must be confusing me with someone else. I don't know you at all. You have no right to accuse me...."

"I'm not accusing anyone, sir," Mr. Marancourt said placidly. "I'm merely saying I recognize you. Yesterday you came into my shop on Bac Street. You were there almost at the same time as this other gentleman," he explained, motioning to Martin. "The day before, he had come into my store asking for an estimate on a silver tankard exactly like the ones you brought. He said he wanted to know how much they were worth just out of curiosity.

"I don't mind telling you," continued Mr. Marancourt, "it was a strange coincidence having identical tankards show up in my shop two days in a row. You see, that sort of thing is very rare these days. You don't see many like them anymore. That's what struck me at the time and why I remember the incident so clearly.

"Anyway, this first gentleman came back the next day wanting to see a pair of stirrups from the twelfth century. I have a very fine collection of these in my shop, a collection I'm very proud of. Anyway, while he was looking at them, I left him alone for a moment to serve yourself, sir," he said, looking at Leo.

He stopped talking and looked around at everyone. Suddenly he seemed awkward and a little embarrassed. "Do these tankards belong to the person who brought them to my store?" he asked, turning to Marthe. "What I mean is, they're not stolen goods, are they? I certainly hope not. I mean, a man of my reputation. . . . You know, anyone in my position is expected to report any suspicious goods to the police immediately."

Martin turned and looked Leo straight in the eye, waiting for him to say something. But Leo, his eyes still fixed on the floor, steadfastly remained silent.

"It's a family matter, sir," Martin said finally. "Please don't upset yourself. Thank you for coming, Mr. Marancourt. You've helped a great deal."

"Well, then, if everything is settled to your satisfaction I'll wait outside in the car until you're ready to go," said the dealer courteously as he picked up the tankards.

"Yes," replied Martin "that will be fine—and thanks again. Oh, if you're in a hurry to return to Paris, please go ahead. We've kept you long enough as it is, and I can always take the train back. I'm grateful to you for the ride here as it is."

Martin shook hands with the antique dealer who nodded politely to Diane and left the room.

As soon as he heard the car drive away, Martin turned to Leo. "Well, at least Mr. Marancourt won't press charges. What are you going to do now, Leo?" he asked quietly.

A little color had returned to Leo's face, and he'd recovered some of his composure. "Would you believe me, Diane, if I said I did it for you? I knew how much difficulty you were having here, and how short of cash you were...."

"You're a thief, Leo...and no, I wouldn't believe you. I believe you stole those tankards for your own profit. I suspect, moreover, that that is why you wanted me to sell Black Oaks. You were going to make sure we were married, then get me to use the money from selling it and its contents for... for your horses. I don't think I can forgive you for that."

"Your grandmother showed us the tankards when we were children," Leo said. "I didn't know how much they were worth then, and I didn't think you would ever sell any of your silver no matter how desperate you were for money."

"And so you timed your theft—or perhaps I should say suddenly recognized your opportunity—when there was a burglar in the area who happened to have a penchant for silver. Right?"

"I did it for you," Leo repeated miserably.

"Somehow, I don't think Diane believes you, Mr. Marchand," Martin interjected coldly.

"Who are you anyway?" Leo said angrily, turning to Martin. "And what business have you barging in, minding our business?"

"Why don't you ask your mother," Martin inquired mildly meeting Leo's icy gaze.

"My mother?" Leo repeated, surprised. "What does she have to do with this?"

"Perhaps that's another question we should ask her," Martin replied levelly. "Well, shall we go? We'll follow in Diane's car."

SOME TEN MINUTES LATER both cars drew up in front of
Wildacres. His anger still smoldering, Leo strode ahead
of Diane and Martin into the house.

"Mother," he called sharply. "There is someone here
who wants to meet you." He paced back and forth until
he heard his mother's step on the stairs.

Irene Marchand came downstairs and gasped as she
saw Martin standing in the front hall.

"You!" she said, her voice a whisper.

"Well, mother," Leo said impatiently, "do you know
this man?"

"You haven't changed since you were a boy, really,"
she said staring at Martin as if at a ghost.

"What is going on between you two?" Leo asked in
exasperation. "Mother, who is this man, for heaven's
sake?"

Mrs. Marchand walked past the three of them standing in the hall and sat down on the living-room sofa.
"I wondered if any of you would be back," she said
softly. "I never really thought we'd get away with
it."

"I admit, you did for a while, Mrs. Marchand—for
fifteen long years in fact."

"Martin, what's this all about?" Diane asked, unable
to follow the conversation.

"Remember I told you that I'd once lived in a house I
loved, and that my parents had to sell it?" asked Martin.

Diane nodded, and he continued. "Well, my father's
company went bankrupt. Embezzlement was suspected, though never proved, and he had to sell everything.
When my parents moved to Brazil, they had nothing
but the clothes they could carry."

"I'm sorry to hear that," Leo cut in harshly, "but I fail to see what that has to do with my mother."

Ignoring Leo, Martin turned back to Mrs. Marchand.

"Your slander and lies and the ruining of my father's business—as well as his good name—have caught up with you now," he said calmly.

"I came to tell you—" Martin's soft words rang clearly in the absolute quiet of the room "—that your husband's bookkeeper died of cancer recently. But perhaps you knew that. What you don't know is that he wanted to die with a clear conscience so he gave us all the information we needed with regard to the embezzlement. I know now it was he who helped you and your husband falsify my father's account books to make it look as if he was the one who embezzled the money and not the three of you. Because of you, my father lost his business, all his money and his good name. But you got off scot-free. My family lawyer, a Mr. Duparc, will be contacting you very soon to discuss these matters in more detail."

When Martin had finished speaking, the silence in the room was palpable.

"Help me upstairs, Leo," Irene Marchand murmured finally. "I'd like to lie down." Without another word, she left the room, holding onto her son's arm for support.

"Shall we go?" Martin said to Diane, putting his arm around her.

"Martin, this is all so unbelievable," Diane said once they were in the car. "I'm astounded...I had no idea...."

"Well, you certainly have a right to an explanation,"

he replied smiling at her. Collecting his thoughts for a minute, he began to talk.

"My mother is Irene Marchand's sister, so you can imagine how close our two families were. I don't want to go into all the painful details, but there are some things I would like you to know. My father was a businessman who owned three factories in the north of France plus a foundry in the east, which was managed by one of his best friends.

"All these enterprises did quite well for a while, but then, when my father was in the middle of modernizing his factories, he ran into some rather serious cash flow problems. He asked his brother-in-law to lend him some money to tide him over. My uncle agreed on condition that my father let him arrange the merger of the three factories and the foundry as one legal entity. From that day on, my father's business went steadily downhill. I was there and saw how desperately he tried to get back on his feet, but it was a losing battle. Despite all his work a lot of people accused him of embezzling funds from his own company. No one could ever prove it— because there was nothing to prove—but the money wasn't there, and finally he was forced to file for bankruptcy. He was a very moral man, and he even sold much of his personal property to pay off his creditors and employees. His friend, the one who ran the foundry, had invested a lot of borrowed capital in the business. He was ruined, too, and died almost immediately afterward from a heart attack.

"I was fourteen when all this happened. I'll never forget it—it was awful. However, my parents were wonderful and showed such courage in the face of adversity that none of us children ever forgot it." He stopped for a moment and looked over at Diane, his face relaxing for a moment into a smile.

"My father knew he was innocent, but he felt deeply ashamed of his failure and blamed himself for his friend's death. And no one would trust him anymore. Finally, he decided to leave the country and start over again. I guess he wanted to get as far away as possible because he chose to move to Brazil." Martin fell silent suddenly and seemed lost in thought.

"More than anyone else," he continued, looking at Diane again, "you can understand how difficult it was for us to leave our country and the home we loved so much. However, none of us ever admitted how upset we were. Our parents couldn't afford to break down in front of the children and, of course, the younger children were so enchanted by the ocean voyage, they didn't fully realize what had happened until much later. And my parents did manage to create a wonderful life for us in a strange country.

"Well, to make a long story short, we'd almost managed to put all the sad memories behind us, when, a few months ago, that bookkeeper from my uncle's office informed us that the merger of the three factories, which was supposed to have been drawn up by my uncle, his wife and some of his colleagues, didn't exist at all. In creating that so-called merger, their one and only goal had been to appropriate my parents' fortune through apparently legal channels. But it was out-and-out robbery. Mr. Marchand only had a modest law practice on the outskirts of Paris, but, as you can see, he had very big ideas.

"At first we thought the bookkeeper's letter was some sort of bad joke. But then, almost on his death-bed, the man wrote to my father again, begging him to come back so the dying man could clear his conscience by giving our family all the papers necessary to prove Marchand's guilt.

"He told my father he would find additional proof if he studied the Marchand's life-style these days. The accountant described the Marchands' apartment in Paris—which they hardly ever used—and their well-staffed château in the country—Wildacres. My uncle had become very wealthy, he said, quite a feat for a lawyer with a small practice. And my aunt was indulging all kinds of extravagance, living in a grand style she couldn't possibly manage on an unknown lawyer's income. The accountant told my father that she had been the one at the bottom of the whole scheme and that he had papers in his possession that she'd signed. He begged him again to come back so he could die in peace."

Martin stopped speaking and turned to look at Diane. "That's how I ended up at Black Oaks that stormy night."

"Are you going to try and get back any of the money the Marchands stole from your father?" Diane asked.

"No, I don't think so," Martin replied, a mocking light in his eyes. "We have plenty of money now. We don't need theirs. But there is the family of my father's friend. The Marchands will definitely have to make restitution to them."

Diane remained silent for the rest of the trip back to Black Oaks. Her mind was whirling with the events of the afternoon, and she was still trying to assimilate all that Martin had told her.

When they were back at Black Oaks, seated in the

living room and sipping a glass of wine, Diane spoke again.

"Martin, you say this happened fifteen years ago. I was ten then, and I seem to remember that the Marchands were just as well off back then as they are now."

"Not at all, Diane, that's just the point. Irene Marchand has always had very expensive tastes, and in order to support what she thought was a fitting lifestyle, her husband went deeply into debt. That's why, I guess, they came up with the idea of embezzlement. My father's business troubles couldn't have come at a better time," he added wryly.

The appetizing smell of a roasting chicken wafted into the living room as Diane sat lost in thought. It brought her out of her reverie, and she turned to Martin with a smile.

"I'd better tell Marthe and Germaine what happened," she said, getting up. With a smile she added, "I trust you'll stay for dinner?" Martin nodded appreciatively and when Diane left the room, there was a flush of pleasure on her face.

Long after dinner was finished, Martin and Diane remained seated at the table, their coffee cups in front of them, the candles in the middle of the table flickering in the soft breeze blowing in through the window.

"Will Leo go to jail, Martin?" Diane asked, idly stirring her coffee.

"That's really up to you, Diane," Martin replied quietly. "He had nothing to do with his parents' crime. You might want to tell him that if he buys the tankards back and returns them to you, you'll let the matter drop."

"I'd think I'd rather do that than call the police," she murmured.

"And now, my lovely," Martin said, walking around the table to her and putting his hands on her shoulders. "Tell your night traveler whether he has to go on walking under the stars searching for his long lost home. Or there is a chance you might accept. . . ."

But Diane didn't let him finish. Getting up from the table, she turned to face him. No sooner had she put her arms around him than his mouth was on hers.

Chapter 18

Diane slept late the next morning. When she got downstairs, she found Martin and Charles in the dining room, deep in conversation.

"Good morning, Miss Diane," Charles said beaming.

"Morning, my lovely," Martin added, gazing appreciatively at her as she walked into the room. Her blond hair gleamed in the sunlight, and her navy blue and white sundress showed her slim, tanned body off to perfection.

"Marthe and Germaine have gone to church, Diane, but there's coffee in the pot on the stove."

"Charles was just telling me about the news he heard on the radio this morning," Martin said when Diane reappeared with her coffee. "It seems the police caught the burglar yesterday afternoon in a pawnshop in Paris. Apparently they'd staked out most of them and caught this fellow red-handed with a number of valuables."

"That's a relief. I certainly hope all the people he

robbed get their possessions back. What news of the estate, Charles?" Diane asked after a pause.

"Things are more or less the same, miss," Charles said. "But even though it's Sunday, I think I'll do my rounds and come back later today to tell you what I've found. I best be off now."

When Charles had gone, Martin refilled his coffee cup and pulled his chair up beside hers.

"A penny for your thoughts," Martin said, seeing a puzzled frown on Diane's face.

"There's something that doesn't add up here, Martin," Diane said, putting down her cup and turning toward him. "If the Marchands are so well off, why did Leo steal the tankards?"

"Uncle Jacques's accountant told me a number of things when I spoke to him, Diane," Martin told her quietly, leaning back in his chair.

"When he wrote to my father admitting his own part in the embezzlement, he indicated that my uncle's finances were in serious trouble. I came to France immediately to talk with him. In fact, I'd just seen him the day before I came to Black Oaks for the first time.

"Anyway," he continued, "apparently Aunt Irene's spending has been wildly extravagant, and when there had been sufficient funds, Uncle Jacques had made little attempt to curtail it. But much of the money had been invested badly, and the combination of that and her voracious spending of the remaining capital has now dragged them into debt on rather a large scale.

"Did Charles tell you about meeting me in the woods that day with my camera?"

Diane nodded.

"Well," Martin continued, "we talked for a while,

and he mentioned Leo's racehorse and his plans for setting up proper stables and hiring trainers. Having spoken to my uncle's accountant, I knew Leo couldn't possibly have the money for such an undertaking."

He stopped talking and Diane interjected, "But how did Charles know about that? Leo had made me promise not to tell a soul."

"It seems that Leo and Gerardy had struck up quite a friendship," Martin continued, "and Charles had heard Leo mentioning it to Gerardy. I guess Charles assumed you knew about it."

"Leo and Gerardy are friends?" Diane repeated in amazement. "Leo knew how much trouble I was having with Gerardy. What could possibly—

"Martin," she interrupted herself suddenly, "I've suddenly remembered something. A few days ago, Charles and I were in the woods and we came across a trapped stag. While Charles was carting it away, I walked over to the road. I was just wandering, waiting for Charles to come back, and who do you think I saw? Leo and Gerardy together in Leo's car. I'd forgotten about that. . . ."

"I don't have an answer to that one, Diane," Martin replied, "but I have a feeling we're not finished with Leo yet, and at some point he may choose to solve that little mystery for us."

"Martin, going back to what you were saying about Leo not being able to finance the training stables. Do you think he was planning to use the money from the sale of Black Oaks to finance the venture?" Comprehension of Leo's grandiose plans began to dawn on Diane. She was appalled at the audacity of his scheme.

"I think that's exactly what Leo had in mind," Martin

said gently. "When you told me you were engaged to Marchand, Diane, I didn't know what to do. I knew that his parents were crooks and that chances were you had no idea about our side of the family, much less the dealings that had gone on. On the one hand, I wanted to tell you, so that in the light of that information you could make up your mind as to whether or not you still wanted to go on with the marriage. But, on the other hand, there were serious moral questions involved."

"So Leo really didn't care at all about my struggling to manage Black Oaks," Diane said, an incredulous look on her face. "All his concern was just so much talk to induce me to sell. . . ."

"Diane," Martin said quietly, taking her hands in his, "I wanted to tell you, but I didn't think I had the right. I had absolutely no proof that Leo was following in his parents' footsteps. And before I even mentioned their inequities, I felt I had to wait until a formal charge was laid against Uncle Jacques. I just hoped desperately that you wouldn't marry Leo before that.

"But then," he continued, "when I found out that Leo had stolen those tankards. . . well, I was certain of his character. And I decided I had to let you know about the whole ugly business."

"I see," said Diane with a shudder.

"Leo hasn't changed much physically or psychologically from when we were boys. We're about the same age, and he's been a sneaky, selfish character as far back as I can remember. When I saw him come into the antique shop yesterday, I just kept my back to him. He was nervous and anxious to get the money for the tankards and get out. I don't suppose he noticed much while he was talking to Mr. Marancourt."

"Are you two going to sit there all morning?" Marthe asked, bustling into the dining room with a tray in her hands.

"Back already, Marthe?" Diane asked in surprise.

"Oh yes, miss, I've been back a good half hour."

"Goodness!" Diane remarked looking at her watch. "It's nearly lunchtime."

"Shall we go into the garden and enjoy the sun for a while?" Martin asked, getting up.

The noonday sun was hot and the air still and fragrant as they strolled through the grounds, arm in arm.

"What did Leo say to you, Diane, that induced you to consider selling this magnificent place?" Martin's voice was gentle, but Diane found herself flushing with shame.

"He told me I'd compromised myself in the eyes of everyone in the community by letting a strange man into my house that night, and. . . ."

"Oh, I see," Martin replied, holding her more closely. "And that stranger could well have been the burglar everyone was looking for, eh? What an incredible sequence of events, and they all fit so perfectly into Leo's devious little scheme. It's amazing."

"You're not going to leave me, are you?" Diane asked impetuously. "Leo is so violent. He gets terribly angry when things don't go the way he wants them to. I'm afraid he. . . ."

"You don't have to be afraid anymore, my love," Martin said quietly. "I'm going over to Wildacres this afternoon to talk to the Marchands. I have a few things I want to settle with them. First of all, they have to make restitution to the family of my father's friend. I'm not going to let them avoid doing that, although my father doesn't want anything for himself. Then I'm going to talk with Leo."

"I wish you wouldn't go over there alone, Martin. I don't trust them."

As he smiled at her fear, she remembered the way he'd smiled the first evening she met him. She longed to see him smile like that again. When he smiled in that special way, she felt so secure, so sure everything was going to be all right. That smile of his was like a mirror that reflected the true inner nature of this man she'd come to love. Thanks to him, Diane knew she would never have to worry about the future or be afraid of anything ever again. She knew now he would always be there when she needed him.

He interrupted her thoughts with a reassurance. "At this point, I don't think the Marchands would dare do anything to make things worse for themselves. Now don't worry about anything—I'll be fine. Trust me."

Trust him, she thought. She couldn't think of anything she would rather do. To trust him to be there, to feel herself enfolded in his strong, gentle arms, to lean against his powerful chest, knowing everything was going to work out. Diane had never felt happier in her whole life. Now she could leave all the difficult decisions up to him. He would be wise and just. He would make sure all his orders were carried out and back them up with the sheer force of his dynamic personality.

"I'm so afraid when you aren't with me," she said quietly.

"Don't worry, darling. All this business will be over soon. I'm going to hurry things along as much as I can and send a cablegram to my father tomorrow."

As if by some unspoken agreement, they both stopped walking and turned to face each other. Slowly Martin put his arms around Diane.

"I love you, Diane . . . no, I adore you, my beautiful Diane. I only wish I'd been here sooner to stop the misery you've been through in the last month or so."

"It's over; let's forget it," Diane murmured, resting her head against Martin's muscular chest. She was filled with a blissful contentment that more than compensated for the painful weeks since her grandmother's death. Her only fear was that perhaps her newfound happiness might not last.

"Diane," Martin said softly, lifting her face to his, "Will you marry me and let me look after you?"

"Oh, Martin," Diane cried, tightening her arms around his neck. "There is nothing in this world I want more than to be your wife and to have you be master of Black Oaks. And Martin—I adore you, too."

When Martin kissed her, Diane's body trembled with desire. Again and again he kissed her, passionately, lovingly, until Diane thought she'd faint with the strength of her emotion.

At length they drew apart, as Marthe's call beckoned them to lunch.

"I wish you wouldn't go over to Wildacres this afternoon," Diane said to Martin during lunch. "I meant it when I said Leo could be violent. Maybe you should give him a chance to calm down."

"If you feel that strongly, my love, I guess I could wait till tomorrow," Martin replied easily.

Diane flashed him a smile of gratitude and lifted her glass in a toast. "To us," she said happily, "and to Black Oaks."

Chapter 19

After a while Diane happily agreed to Martin's suggestion that they go for a walk on the property.

"I've never really had a look at it," Martin said teasingly. "Don't think I'm looking for a chance to be alone with you!"

Arm in arm they walked into the back garden and down toward the forest. "Tell me about yourself, Martin," Diane said, turning to him. "I really don't know anything about you."

When they reached the pond, they sat down on the sloping hill that dropped down to the water's edge. The grass was covered with pine needles that had dropped from the trees overhead, trees that arched over them like a huge parasol. As they sat together in silence they gazed at the dappled water, soft and black.

"My name isn't Martin Leblanc," Martin began. "That was just a name I made up the first night we met. I didn't want the Marchands to know I was here and I wasn't sure whether you knew them or not at that point. My real name is Martin Lambert. I have a brother William, who is twenty-four and twin sisters, Veronica and Frances, just younger than he. My youngest brother, Bernard, is almost twenty now.

"When our family left France, we had to build a completely new life for ourselves, and we were practically penniless. My parents hadn't left one debt unpaid when they left for Brazil. They didn't own anything anymore, but they didn't owe anyone anything, either. You can't begin to imagine how all this had affected my father. He wasn't the kind of man who took that kind of thing lightly. He was an honorable man of great integrity. And my mother, well...."

He stopped talking for a moment, a faraway look in his eyes.

"Everyone in our family owes her so much," Martin resumed softly. "Everything we are is because of her. She's a wonderful, compassionate, understanding woman. If there were days—and I'm sure there were—when she felt tired or ready to give up, she never said a word about it, and, of course, we never suspected. She was always smiling."

He smiled as he continued, "Everyone came to my mother with problems, and she would always do everything in her power to resolve them with tact and diplomacy. Nothing was ever too difficult for her to tackle. She has a great way with people and they love her. As you can imagine, she was a tremendous help to my father, supporting him and encouraging him as he tried to build a new life for us all. She was the center of our lives and fostered in us a love of life and a sense of personal integrity. She took great joy in being alive, and in spite of the difficult times we faced, she filled us with a hope and optimism.

"When we got to Brazil, we started out on a little ranch about three hours from Brasília. Our first house was very small, but it was always comfortable. Since then, our fortunes have improved somewhat, and now the house is a large ranch-style affair, with a wide balcony on three sides. There is a lawn and all sorts of trees, planted painstakingly, I assure you. We've got eucalyptus trees—they grow very quickly—cypresses and silver poplars. They're beautiful now, but let me tell you, we had the devil's own time getting them to grow. Brazil is a beautiful country, but. . . . The ants—millions of them—invade like an army and devastate everything they can eat their way through. Then there's the wind, which often reaches gale force. But I won't bore you with all that. What's important is that the ranch is beautiful now, something that my parents are justifiably proud of.

"I think I've talked enough. Aren't you falling asleep?"

But Diane was spellbound. "I could listen to you talk forever," she reassured him.

She loved hearing him talk like this, and as he spoke she somehow felt closer to his family—as if she already knew them personally. She was thrilled at the idea that soon the Lambert family would be related to her and that the ties that Martin was establishing now between his family and herself would grow stronger over the years. With the dawning realization of how much she had been alone all her life, Diane could only marvel at the change that was about to take place after the wedding. Black Oaks would be the busy hive of activity that Germaine and Marthe had once described it as being. Shouts and laughter...music and singing. Black Oaks was going to come alive again.

"Tell me more about your land in Brazil," she urged, sensing his pride in his family's adaptation to a new environment.

"Well, it's grazing land, as you know...beautiful in a strange, rugged way. Very different from here." He gestured toward the rolling, verdant fields and the forest beyond.

"The three hundred acres we started out with," he explained, "soon expanded and changed as the house did. Today we have about eight thousand acres of grazing land where we raise about six thousand sheep. They're the best breeds you can get and we're very proud of them."

"Is it very isolated?" asked Diane. "Did you have to go away to school?" Suddenly she wanted to know the smallest details about Martin's life.

"My father was concerned about our education, naturally," Martin replied. "He was aware, of course, that we lived some distance from a town—or village for that matter and realized that initially, anyway, he would have to teach us at home. Every morning, I remember, he would set aside a certain number of hours to teach us. He taught well and somehow managed to both stimulate and sustain our interest in math and geography and so on. I think we all turned out quite well," Martin said, a twinkle in his eye. "Not an ignoramus among us!"

Martin was quiet for a minute or two, staring into the black depths of the pond.

"I never forgot France, you know," he said briskly,

as if for some obscure reason he might be thought disloyal to his birthplace. "Perhaps the move came at a difficult age for me," he offered by way of explanation. "Believe me, Diane, Brazil is a fabulous country: parts of it are wild—totally untamed—and parts of it are modern and sophisticated. Either way it's an astoundingly beautiful country. But France...well, it holds something special for me. I guess it will always be my home for just that reason.

"Do you know, I used to dream of lush farmland like this." He indicated the surrounding acres of Black Oaks with a wide sweep of his arm.

"When the letter arrived from Uncle Jacques's bookkeeper, it hit us all like a bomb. My parents' first thought was that the family's good name would be restored—not so much for their own sake as for us children. And William and my twin sisters were delighted for my father's sake. Veronica has been wanting to come back to France anyway. Only Bernard, my youngest brother, seemed less than thrilled by the news. He hardly remembers France, and he loves his life on the ranch and doesn't want to give it up for anything."

"And how did you feel when the letter came?" she asked softly.

"Me?" he asked, smiling in the way she loved so much. "The first thing I thought of was that I could go back to France. And now that I'm here, I have no intention of going back to Brazil. There's no way I would take you away from your lovely old home, even for a visit just now. So, I'll just have to get some of my family to come here—if you agree that is."

"Oh, Martin, that would be wonderful. Black Oaks

is certainly big enough to accommodate everyone," she replied excitedly.

"I wonder what my family will say when they get my letter telling them all the news?" Martin said, smiling.

"My grandmother always dreamed of the time when Black Oaks would be full of people again. She longed for the old days when the house was full of life and laughter. Grandmother loved everything that was alive, that moved, laughed, cried. She was full of life herself and loved to feel it around her.

"But there were only the two of us and we couldn't quite fill the bill. I was happy enough because I had her, and that was all I needed. Every once in a while I realized the house was much too big for just the two of us, but it didn't bother me the way it did her." Diane smiled ruefully, then continued. "I know she hated the silence that filled the house all the last years of her life. She was terribly lonely, but I couldn't do much to fill the void for her. She needed so much more.

"I think that's why she was so eager for me to marry," Diane added softly. "She wanted my children to fill up Black Oaks."

A gentle breeze blew across the pond, rippling the water into miniscule waves.

"Wouldn't it be wonderful if your whole family left Brazil and came back to France to live? If Bernard really loves the pampas, maybe he'll want to stay there. But the rest of them could buy a property in this area and live close to us here at Black Oaks."

Diane felt a strange sensation flood through her as she said the word "us." It seemed to draw her even closer to Martin than before.

She fell silent and didn't dare face him directly. All

she could see of him were his long legs stretched out in front of him.

Suddenly she heard him laugh softly, and before she knew it, he had put his arm around her and pulled her close.

"Diane," he said simply.

After a moment, he gently held her from him. "It's amazing how a man's whole life can be summed up in a woman's name, isn't it? Diane," he repeated, then brought his lips down on hers.

Chapter 20

Shortly after dinner, while Diane and Martin were going over some accounts in the study, Charles knocked on the door.

"Excuse me, miss," he said breathlessly, "but I caught one of the village boys taking a rabbit out of a trap. He's in the kitchen; I thought you'd want to talk to him. Should I bring him in here, miss?"

"Thank you, Charles. Yes, please bring him in." Diane turned to Martin in consternation.

"I'll handle this, darling," he said quietly.

When Charles returned he had with him a sullen boy, about fifteen years old, in faded pair of blue jeans and a stained T-shirt.

"The gamekeeper tells us that he caught you taking a rabbit out of a trap. Is that true?" Martin asked the boy calmly.

The boy looked at the floor and said nothing.

"Do you deny it?" Martin asked, a little more firmly.

"Well, he saw me, didn't he?" the boy answered belligerently.

"How long have you been poaching in this forest?" was the next question.

"Not long."

"How long, I asked?"

"A few months," the boy mumbled, his gaze reverting from Martin to the floor.

"How many of you are there?"

"How many of who?" the boy returned rudely.

"How many in your gang of poachers," Martin said evenly.

"Five. . .six, maybe."

"Was it your idea, or did someone put you up to it?"

"I don't know what you're jumping on me for," the boy said aggressively. "Why don't you talk to that other guy, the guy that works here? He's the one who's in charge."

Martin raised his eyebrows in surprise. "Just whom do you mean?" he asked quietly.

"The big guy—the guy that throws his weight around all the time. Gerard or something."

"Gerardy!" Diane gasped, leaning forward in her chair.

"Charles, please see if Gerardy's at his house or anywhere around the estate. If you can find him, tell him I want to see him immediately."

"What's your name, boy?" Martin asked the lad when Charles had gone.

"Rene."

"Rene what?"

"Rene Gilbert."

"Sit down, Rene, you'll be here for a little while longer." The boy shuffled over to an armchair. When Charles returned with Gerardy, the overseer started when he saw the boy sitting there.

"What the—" he began, then stopped, a deep flush spreading over his face and neck.

"Do you know each other?" Martin asked calmly.

"That's the guy," Rene said, jumping up. "He's the one that's in charge."

"Would you like to tell us about it, Gerardy?" Martin asked coolly.

Various expressions flashed across Gerardy's features, as if he were trying to figure out his best line of defense. There was no sign of his previous haughtiness; he looked sullen, beaten.

"It was Mr. Marchand's idea," he muttered finally. "He said I didn't have to do any poaching myself, but he'd make it worth my while if I made sure there was a lot of poaching going on."

"Did he say why?" Diane cut in.

"He said you didn't realize you couldn't manage the estate, but that if the poaching was stepped up, maybe you'd give in and sell the place."

"So, in exchange for a certain amount of money, you've been making sure that the forest was always full of poachers, is that it?" Martin asked casually.

"Yes, sir."

"And once the forest was full of poachers, you thought that maybe you'd just take a little game yourself from time to time, right? Never minding that it was both against the law and a clear violation of your contract?"

"I never—"

"Excuse me, Gerardy," Martin interrupted, reaching into his pocket. "I don't believe you."

Martin walked over to the farmer and handed him a photograph. Diane noticed the color suffuse his face once again.

"Martin," Diane whispered, "let me see that picture."

He handed it over. It was quite unmistakeably a picture of Gerardy pulling a rabbit out of a trap. Leo stood beside him. A No Trespassing sign to one side bore the unmistakable legend, "Black Oaks," and the developer's date on the print was very recent.

"Charles, phone the game wardens, please," Diane said crisply. "I think we have all the proof we need."

It seemed like ages to Diane before the wardens arrived. By the time they left, taking Gerardy and the young boy with them, she was exhausted.

"I don't think I can take any more," she said half joking to Martin as the two of them sat in the living room, rehashing the events of the last couple of days.

"Leo really stooped that low to force me to sell Black Oaks! And to think I was going to marry that man," she added, shaking her head. "It's incredible."

"I should have told you about that picture earlier, Diane, forgive me, but I only got the print this morning. I didn't want to say anything until I knew the photograph had come out—I hadn't been sure how much detail the telephoto lens would have picked up."

"I guess that's the proof I need to break Gerardy's contract without his making any trouble?" Diane said, leaning back on the sofa, her eyes closed.

"Yes, you have a clear-cut case on that score," Martin agreed. "Come on, it's late. Time for us to say good-bye to this day."

Taking Diane's hand, he gently pulled her to her feet. "Good night, darling. Sleep well. I think I'll sleep in the study tonight instead of the guest room upstairs. I don't know if they'll hold Gerardy or not. If he's released on bail, I don't want him coming back up to the house making trouble."

The moon threw a brilliant shaft of light into Diane's bedroom. Instead of keeping the shutters open as she usually did, she decided to close them so that she wouldn't be awakened by the sun in the morning. With a yawn she crawled into bed, falling asleep as soon as her head touched the pillow.

It seemed as though she'd only been asleep for a minute or two when she heard a scratching sound. Puzzled rather than frightened, she sat up in bed as she tried to pinpoint the source of the noise.

"Diane," a voice called softly, and a few seconds later she heard her name repeated. Again the scratching sound came.

Jumping out of bed, she went over to the window and opened the shuters. Leo was standing directly below the window, a handful of pebbles in one hand.

"What are you doing here," she called in a loud whisper. "Go away."

"Listen to me," he called, his words slurred. "Let me in, I can explain everything." He lurched back a step as he spoke.

The man's drunk, Diane thought with distaste. She drew her head back in and had begun to close the shuters when Leo called out again, making no attempt to keep his voice quiet.

"I said listen to me, you heartless. . . ."

"For heaven's sake, keep your voice down, Leo," Diane said as loudly as she dared. "You'll wake everyone up. Now, go home. . . please."

"Just give me a chance to talk to you," he screamed, lurching back again.

"That will do, Leo," Martin said quietly, coming up behind him. "The lady said go home."

"You!" Leo said thickly, spinning around lopsidedly to stare at Martin. "Why you. . . ."

Taking a revolver out of his jacket, he fired at Martin.

Diane screamed in horror. Grabbing her housecoat, she flew down the stairs and out the front door.

Martin and Leo were struggling on the ground. As she reached the bottom of the steps, Martin knocked Leo unconscious and took the gun out of his hand.

"Martin, are you all right?" she gasped, terrified. "I thought he'd killed you!"

"Fortunately his aim wasn't too good," Martin replied breathlessly. "Thank goodness, he was drunk. He's strong and is probably quite a good marksman when he's sober."

They both turned to look at Leo, who lay sprawled, unconscious, on the ground. Diane shivered and buried her head in Martin's shoulder.

"Go inside, darling," he said. "I'll be in in a minute."

As Diane went inside, the ground floor lights suddenly came on, and Charles and Marthe scurried down the hall, their dressing gowns flapping.

"What happened, miss?" Charles asked, his voice full of concern. "We heard a shot. . . ."

"Everything's fine, Charles," Diane smiled wearily. "Just another nocturnal visitor!"

AN HOUR LATER, Diane, Martin and the three servants were sitting in the kitchen drinking coffee. All of them had resigned themselves to not getting any sleep that night.

Martin had explained to the others what had happened, and now they were discussing it excitedly. Germaine asked a stream of questions, quite obviously enjoying the drama.

After exchanging a look with Martin, Diane signaled them all to stop talking. "I have an announcement for you," she said self-consciously, feeling the color rise to her cheeks. "Martin has asked me to marry him, and. . .I've accepted."

"Oh, miss, that's wonderful!" Marthe cried, rushing over to embrace her. "I'm so happy for you!"

"Congratulations, miss," Charles added gruffly.

"I'm not surprised," was all Germaine said, a self-satisfied look on her face. "Not surprised at all. Welcome to Black Oaks, Mister Martin."

"This calls for a toast," Marthe called, scuffling off to fetch a bottle of wine.

Ignoring Charles and Germaine, Martin walked over to Diane and pulled her to her feet. Folding her in his arms, he pulled her face up to his. He kissed her deeply and sensuously, and when Marthe returned with the wine, they were oblivious to everything but their own happiness and the joy they'd found in each other.

Chapter 21

Several days had gone by. Diane was in the garden, lovingly tending her flowers. As she pruned the geraniums, she found herself humming the tune of an old song whose words she had long forgotten. She felt light-hearted, at peace with herself and her surroundings, free from all the misery and turmoil of the last few months.

In a huge pine tree nearby, a blackbird was singing its heart out, and Diane's spirits soared with the sheer joy of being alive. She smiled as she thought back over the extraordinary events that had led up to this newfound happiness. Everything seemed so perfect that at times she seriously wondered if it could last.

A flock of swallows fluttered up into the air and broke the silence of the oncoming twilight. Attracted by their sudden movement, Diane looked up and followed them with her eyes until they were out of sight. Their nests were in one of the farm buildings. Seeing the swallows reminded Diane of the flurry of activity going on in the house.

How busy they'd all been earlier today! It was as if Black Oaks was waking up after a very long, deep sleep. Energy was beginning to course through the house again. All the windows had been thrown open as part of a thorough cleaning job that was being carried out by Marthe and Germaine with the assistance of two girls from the village. All four were busily preparing rooms for Mrs. Lambert, William and the twins who were expected to arrive for an extended visit within the month.

Diane had opened the well-stocked cupboards and chosen the best bed linens and tablecloths for her overseas visitors. All the upholstery covers had been scrubbed, and the antique wooden furniture waxed and rubbed to a soft sheen.

Marthe had left the confines of her kitchen to supervise all the preparations. She went from room to room seeing that the village girls missed no speck of dust, the furniture was at its best, the curtains perfectly crisp.

"I think we should put Mrs. Lambert in grandmother's old room," Diane announced, "and the twins in the green and blue rooms. Now William... where do you think we should put him, Germaine?"

"Why don't we put him in your father's old room," Marthe offered, more as a statement than a suggestion. "It's in good condition, even if it does need a really good cleaning. All those shut-up rooms do; they haven't been used in years. Let's clean a few more bedrooms while we're at it—there might be more visitors, who knows?"

Marthe sighed contentedly. "It'll be marvelous to

have the place filled with people again, won't it, Germaine? Just like the old days."

"Miss Diane, in my whole life, I never saw such comings and goings as we had when your father and grandfather were around. During hunting season, the house was packed to the brim. It was wonderful," Germaine said, her eyes misty with nostalgia.

"There must have been hordes of people then," one of the village girls exclaimed. "There seem to be endless bedrooms."

"Only ten," Germaine replied, as if describing an average-size house. "I remember we'd have to put some of the guests up in the study and the library. I hope things are going back to the way they used to be, miss. Marthe and I used to love all the activity."

"Are Mister Martin's father and other brother coming as well?" the village girl asked.

"They're coming just for the wedding," Germaine replied. "They'll only be here a few days, I expect. I guess they can't leave their ranch in Brazil untended for too long."

"I'm going to try to make Mr. Lambert stay longer," Diane said, a mischievous twinkle in her eye. "His youngest brother, Bernard, is apparently quite able to take over running the ranch for a month or so."

Standing among the geraniums, Diane recalled these happy plans and thought about Martin's dream of seeing Bernard taking charge of the ranch, which he apparently loved with the same emotion she felt for Black Oaks. . . .

A loud, energetic footstep on the garden path brought Diane's attention back to her surroundings, and she turned in the direction of the sound. In the gathering dusk, all she could see was Martin's tall, slim silhouette outlined against the sky.

He stood there for a minute, then quickly walked toward her. He had just returned from the farm where he had spent the afternoon making a complete inventory of all the machinery, livestock and produce that belonged to the estate.

With a sudden gesture she threw a bunch of faded roses into the bushes and went running to meet him. This was the new master of Black Oaks, the man to whom she'd entrusted everything she cared for most in the world. He opened his arms wide, caught her to him and held her close. She leaned against his broad chest, her eyes closed, and savored the magic of the moment.

As they stood in each other's arms, the silence hovered over them as if nature herself wanted to contribute to the moment by preventing a single sound from disturbing their bliss, as if she knew the price that had been paid for this moment of loving peace and wanted to give the two lovers her silent blessing.

4 FREE

MYSTIQUE BOOKS

Your FREE gift includes . . .

Exciting novels of romance, suspense and drama, with intriguing characters and surprising plot twists, set against international backgrounds.

PROPER AGE FOR LOVE, *Claudette Jaunière*
Anne didn't understand when her fiancé suggested she become his mistress — not his wife. And so she fled across Europe into a nightmare of intrigue and danger where her very survival depended on the man she most loved — and feared.

ISLAND OF DECEIT, *Alix André*
Determined to discover her sister's fate on an exotic Caribbean isle, Rosalie finds herself enmeshed in a web of lies, dangerously attracted to the only man who might know the dreadful truth.

HIGH WIND IN BRITTANY, *Caroline Gayet*
What elaborate charade of identity was the stranger playing on the tiny coastal town? Only Marie knew, and her knowledge brought her danger.

HOUSE OF SECRETS, *Denise Noël*
Would Pascale reveal a family secret kept hidden for years . . . or stand accused of murdering another woman to protect the man she loved?

Your FREE gift includes

House of Secrets—by Denise Noël
Proper Age for Love—by Claudette Jaunière
Island of Deceit—by Alix André
High Wind in Brittany—by Caroline Gayet

Mail this coupon today!

What readers
say about
Mystique Books...